Saleni Hopkins

Within the Purdah

In the Zenana homes of Indian princes, and Heroes and heroines of Zion

Saleni Hopkins

Within the Purdah
In the Zenana homes of Indian princes, and Heroes and heroines of Zion

ISBN/EAN: 9783337195007

Printed in Europe, USA, Canada, Australia, Japan

Cover: Foto ©Andreas Hilbeck / pixelio.de

More available books at **www.hansebooks.com**

Salini Armstrong-Hopkins.

WITHIN THE PURDAH

ALSO

In the Zenana Homes of Indian Princes

AND

Heroes and Heroines of Zion

BEING THE PERSONAL OBSERVATIONS OF A MEDICAL
MISSIONARY IN INDIA

By

S. ARMSTRONG-HOPKINS, M.D.

FORMERLY PHYSICIAN IN CHARGE TO THE WOMAN'S HOSPITAL, DISPENSARY,
AND TRAINING SCHOOL FOR NURSES, OF HYDERABAD, SINDH,
UNDER ENGLISH GOVERNMENT APPOINTMENT

NEW YORK: EATON & MAINS
CINCINNATI: CURTS & JENNINGS

PREFACE

DEAR FRIENDS, I know I have done a very
unfashionable thing in harrowing up your
feelings by the recital of some heartrending facts.
Facts, indeed, they are, for each particular case
which I have cited is a real case. In every instance
I have had some particular patient in mind, and
have given you the exact details and history of that
particular patient; and yet each of these particular
patients is but a sample of many similar cases such
as I treated again and again during my dispensary
life. I know that returned missionaries love to
cite instances of natives coming from distant villages to the mission inquiring the way of salvation.
They love to describe revival efforts in country
towns, where, perhaps, the whole village has been
brought to the foot of the cross. All this can be
done. All this is true. The cause of God is making
wonderful strides in that strange, dark land. I, too,
could tell of similar cases of conversions from darkest heathendom; even of Hindu priests who have
left all and chosen affliction with the people of God
rather than to continue the worship of idols; but,
dear friends, I have chosen to tell you these more
unpleasant facts. I have done it deliberately and
"with malice aforethought." At every opportu-

nity I desire to make known these facts to the
people of my own country. Why? Because I
believe in them; I believe in the chivalry of my
own countrymen. Because I believe in my coun-
trywomen and in the children of my native land.
Because I am convinced that the religion of Jesus
Christ, as professed and lived by the people of this
blessed country, is not a farce; is not a mere garment intended for Sunday wear, which is put off
and on at discretion. I believe that you who profess to love the Lord Jesus Christ, who have taken
his name upon yourselves, do partake of his nature
who left his Father's throne and his Father's house
and came to earth—the great Medical Missionary—
to help, and to heal, and to save his people. When
I was in India, and from day to day witnessed such
horrible sights, and heard from the pale, trembling
lips of wee sufferers heartrending stories such as
I have here depicted, I resolved that, if God spared
my life and permitted me again to visit my own
native land, I would raise the purdah of these
zenana homes; I would acquaint the people of this
country with the real condition of the women and
children of that dark continent. For I am sure
that you need but for one short hour to gaze upon
the wretchedness, to look down, as I have looked,
into the depths of these dark places where women
and children, in utter helpnessness, crouch in pain and
woe such as beggar description—that you need only
to see with another's eyes—in order to stir your Christian hearts to do something to relieve; something

to save. I believed, and I do believe, that for you to know is to do. That you who have felt the thrill which comes from the heart of the All Father in the secret place of prayer, who have reached up and taken hold of the omnipotent hand of God in your secret closets, need but to know the facts in order to run with swift feet to deliver, in order to reach out glad, helping hands to lift up, in order to be willing to sacrifice somewhat of your luxuries, somewhat of your comforts, somewhat, perhaps, of those things which you call the necessities of life, in order to do your part toward sending the Gospel message to those people who sit in darkness and see no light; remembering that inasmuch as you do it unto one of the least of these, you do it unto him.

Do you remind me that I have already confessed that medicine and surgery and all that the English government can accomplish by establishing great hospitals throughout India are of comparatively little avail, and cannot fully meet the needs of these people, because the tortures arising from mental and spiritual conditions are so much greater than any physical suffering? That their customs and barbarous practices are so deeply rooted that nothing can overthrow them? True; but, dear friends, I am glad to add that there is one remedy—one remedy—and only one. It is the blessed Gospel of Jesus Christ, and *it is sufficient*. Send it to them. Send out your missionaries with God's word. Let them go to these suffering women and children, and tell the story of the love of God and of the love of Christ for them. Their hearts are aching and bleeding and famishing for love. In their lives they have never known it; never felt it. They have no hope of anything better beyond the grave. Send this glad, beautiful message; send it quickly. They will embrace it; they will receive it; they will forsake all for it. And when once they do accept this blessed Gospel message all these shackles of superstition, heathen beliefs, prejudices, and barbarous practices will fall off, and they will arise in all the emancipated freedom and liberty of glad children of God. Nothing but this can meet the case. God's word is a sufficient remedy. Won't you take it? Won't you send it? Won't you sacrifice something in order to do this? O, do it! In the name of God Almighty, in the name of the Lord Jesus Christ, whom you love and revere, I entreat you to send the Gospel to these poor women and children, and to send it quickly!

SINDH

The gloom that here is found
    Is like to that of Hell;
While ghastly specters 'round
    The bravest spirit quell.
O God, thou Source of light,
    This darkness all dispel;
Drive back the heathen's night,
    Till they thy praise shall swell.
                    Amen.

CONTENTS

BOOK III

HEROES AND HEROINES OF ZION

CONCLUSION

BY THE REV. GEORGE F. HOPKINS, A.M.

LIST OF ILLUSTRATIONS

BOOK I
WITHIN THE PURDAH

---

*"And the King shall answer and say unto them,
Verily I say unto you, Inasmuch as ye have done it
unto one of the least of these my brethren, ye have
done it unto me."*—MATTHEW xxv, 40.

2

BOOK I

WITHIN THE PURDAH

THE native of Hindustan—the Hindu, the Mohammedan, the Parsee, the Eurasian, but, perhaps, more particularly the Hindu—has somehow acquired a reputation throughout Europe, and doubtless in America as well, for possessing by nature all those attributes and characteristics which we in this Christian land have learned to regard as emanating from the Spirit of God alone, and which we expect to find more often and more fully exemplified in the lives of those who live nearest to the Lord Jesus Christ and who partake most of his nature. The Hindu is supposed to be, of all creatures on earth, the most generous, the most kind-hearted, the most gentle, the most sympathetic, and the most unselfish. After living for nearly seven years in India I must tell you that the reverse of this is true. The great principle which we, as Christians, were taught at our mother's knee holds true. Charity, kindness, unselfishness, thoughtful consideration for others, love, and tenderness, emanate in large measure from God, and from him only, and those who live nearest to him and walk most closely in the footsteps of our Lord Jesus Christ do most fully exemplify these characteristics.

17

It has been said that among the many languages spoken by the peoples of Hindustan there is no such word as home, in the sense in which we understand it; that among all the languages spoken there is no such word as love, in the sense in which we know it. I cannot vouch for the truth of this, as I am not acquainted with the languages of India, but I do know that among all the heathen people of that country there is no such place as home, as we understand it; there is no such sentiment as love, as we feel it. And yet it is not difficult to understand how the Hindu has gained the reputation of being all that we have mentioned—kind-hearted, gentle, loving, etc.

Those who attended the Parliament of Religions at our great Columbian Exposition may have heard some educated, proud Brahman declare before the civilized nations of the world that the Hindu religion is better than the Christian religion, because it inculcates such kindness of heart and gentleness of nature as to render its follower incapable of stretching forth his hand to slay any living creature. This same proud Brahman, true to his training in deceit and misrepresentation, did not further explain why the Hindu refuses to slay even the creeping thing which crosses his pathway or the deadly serpent which imperils his life. At the first glance his statement has a seeming truthfulness. There is a trite saying to the effect that a half truth, or a lie which contains a partial truth, is the worst kind of a lie. It is true that a Hindu will not, under any circumstance, put any living thing to death. If you lived in India, and a venomous serpent, whose sting is death in twenty minutes—and without remedy—were to cross your threshold, you might call in vain upon your Hindu servant to slay that serpent. He would fall at your feet and declare his willingness to serve you to the utmost of his ability, but would beg you to forgive him for refusing to kill the serpent which threatens your life.

There are three explanations of the foregoing fact, the first of which seems almost to bear out our educated Brahman in his statement concerning the superiority of the Hindu as compared with the Christian religion. In the religious history of the Hindu, after a reign of terror in which the priests are said to have "multiplied religious ceremonies and made ritual the soul of worship," and when "sacrifice assumed still more and more exaggerated forms, becoming more protracted, more expensive, more bloody—a hecatomb of victims was but a small offering," came a time when "the tension seemed too great, and the bow snapped. Buddhism arose. We may call this remarkable system the product of the age—an inevitable rebellion against intolerable sacerdotalism; and yet we must not overlook the importance of the very distinct and lofty personality of Buddha (Sakya Muni) as a power molding it into shape." Buddha effected a vast revolution in Indian thought. "My law," said he, "is a law of mercy for all." In the forefront of his religious system he put certain great fundamental principles of morality; he made religion consist in duty rather than in rites, and reduced duty, for the most part, to mercy and kindness toward all living creatures. This did away with all slaughter of animals. The people, having grown weary of priestcraft and ritualism, gladly embraced the teachings of this great reformer. This religious system was, in fact, a rebound or reaction from the excessive cruelties which had preceded it.

The second explanation is found in the fact that the Hindu worships a large number of animals, and would not naturally be disposed to slay the object of his worship. It is a common thing to see a Hindu doing poojah (worship) to the ants by the wayside, and bringing flour or boiled rice with which to feed them. They are his gods. He also worships the serpent, the monkey, the bull, and many other animals.

The third explanation may be traced as follows: The Hindu religion leads its follower to believe in the transmigration of souls; therefore a Hindu will not kill the ant which crosses his path in the street, or the deadly serpent, or the venomous scorpion, or the rabid dog which has torn the limbs of his own child, not because of kind-heartedness on the part of this same Hindu, but because by so doing he fears he may slay his deceased mother-in-law, or great aunt, or second cousin, or some other near and dear relative whose spirit is at this time

The Punjapole Asylum for Animals

inhabiting the body of this serpent, scorpion, or rabid dog; and for this great crime he may, in some future state of existence, be doomed to occupy the body of this same creature which he has wickedly put to death.

One of the practical outgrowths of this religious belief may be seen in the city of Bombay, in the establishment of an asylum or place of refuge where all diseased, maimed, decrepit, aged, or otherwise dangerous animals may be confined. Just as the English government provides places of refuge for unfortunate mortals afflicted with leprosy, cholera, smallpox, and insanity, so have the high-caste Brahmans of Bombay established such an asylum or hospital for animals. However, one can hardly speak of it correctly as either an asylum or a hospital, because there is no effort made to restore these inmates to health, to prolong their lives, or to promote their comfort. It is merely a place of banishment where offensive or harmful domestic animals are kept until they die, in order that no Brahman may be compelled in self-protection to put any of these creatures to death, and so bring a curse upon his own soul. This same Brahman will beat his domestic animals most cruelly starve and torture them in many ways, thus exhibiting his lack of kindness. Indeed, you need only to acquaint yourself with the inner home-life of the Hindu, you need only to pass in behind the purdah of his zenana home and behold his conduct toward the members of his own household, in order to know for yourself that my first proposition is true, and that the Hindu is of all people the most cowardly and the most cruel; for a cruel man is always a coward, and a coward is always cruel. In order that you may know the Hindu personally, become acquainted with the members of his family, and understand the principles which govern his life, I shall invite you to accompany me to the English government hospital of Hyderabad, Sindh.

You know about the splendid work that has been done for India by the English government through the efforts of that beautiful woman, the Countess of Dufferin, in establishing government hospitals in all the great cities of that empire. Beautiful hospitals they are; thoroughly equipped with all modern improvements, conveniences, instruments, and apparatus such as you find in the best English hospitals of to-day, having an efficient staff of officers—servants, nurses, compounder or druggist, clerk, interpreter, house surgeon—and at the head of all, the English or American lady physician in charge. It was to such a position as this in the Woman's Hospital, Dispensary, and Training School for Nurses, of Hyderabad, Sindh, that I was called in January, 1893.

Before proceeding further allow me to state that most of the fashions, heathen customs, prejudices, and barbarous practices which I shall here describe are peculiar to the district of Sindh, and would not hold true if applied to the people of Bombay, Calcutta, Madras, or perhaps to any other people of India.

Her Excellency the Countess of Dufferin

Sindh is a province in the northwestern part of British India, having an area of 56,632 square miles and, in 1891, a population of 2,900,000.

Hyderabad is the historical capital of Sindh and chief city of that province. It stands three and a half miles east of the left bank of the Indus River. Its population in 1891 was 58,048, of whom 23,000 were Mohammedans, the remainder being, for the most part, Hindus; unlike the great native city of Hyderabad, Deccan, which is purely Mohammedan, and a walled city.

Our hospital building is a fine brick structure of but one story, surrounded by a very deep veranda, which is shut in from outside gaze by broad pillars, with close lattice work intervening, and over all the Indian chick—a sort of curtain made from split bamboo or reed grass. To this hospital and dispensary come patients representing all classes and castes, rich and poor, Hindu, Mohammedan, and Eurasian. Not only do they come from Hyderabad city, but also from the country villages round about, ten, twenty, thirty, forty, fifty miles distant. Some of the poorer classes from these country villages come walking. I have often seen a little frail woman, weak and ill, who had walked a distance of forty miles from her country village to the hospital—not alone; one never goes alone through the jungles of India. It would not be safe to do so on account of the wild beasts which prowl about and the many venomous and deadly serpents which infest the plains.

It generally happens in a country village that some peer or wealthy native—one of the aristocracy of the place—has a son who is ill. Perhaps he would scarcely undertake such a journey for the sake of a wife or a daughter, but his son, whose life is far more valuable than the life of any woman could be, is ill. There are no hospitals in the country villages, and no English physicians, or even properly educated native doctors. He determines, therefore, to make a trip to the government hospital at Hyderabad, and forthwith proceeds to gather together all the sick people in his village until a large company has arranged to make the journey. Those who are most ill, sons, wives, and daughters of the wealthier members of the community, make the journey on camels, while the poorer people, men, women, and children, and also, perhaps, a large number of strong men, even though of the wealthier class, and high caste, will travel on foot. It is a great sight to see such a caravan *en route* from some distant village to Hyderabad city. The camels, with their slow and measured tread, you may see in the distance, marching single file. The head camel is ridden by one man, who holds one end of a little string not much larger than the cord with which your groceries are bound. The further end of this string is attached to the outer swell of a little wooden nose ring, very much the shape of a thread spool with a very thin stem, which passes through the right nostril of the great docile beast. This nose ring and slender cotton cord serve the

purpose of halter, bridle, and all. A slight tightening of this cord will indicate to the camel that the rider wishes to turn, and a tap on his great neck will serve to guide him in the right direction. The second camel has a similar nose ring, to which is attached a similar cord, this cord being tied to the tail of the first camel; and thus all the twenty-five or fifty camels are tied together, noses and tails, and all with a string so slender that you would think a toss of the head would break it. All the camels except the first one described, which leads the others, are loaded with the women, children, and sick people of the company, while their robust friends and neighbors follow after on foot. The journey is begun late in the afternoon, as soon as the heat of the day begins to abate; and they travel all night, until the morning sun grows so intensely hot as to render further travel hazardous to their lives. Then, if possible, they find a tree with broad, expanded branches, in the shade of which they rest until evening, when they start on again. So it is that early, early in the morning, often before the dawn of day, such a caravan as this arrives at our hospital in Hyderabad. At a signal or a word from the man who sits upon the first camel all these gentle brutes kneel down in the fashion peculiar to themselves, slowly lowering the closed carriages, or baskets, which are loaded with human freight. Then four men—fathers, husbands, or brothers of the occupants of this particular carriage—approach the second camel, and with two long poles attached to its floor raise it (the carriage) to the level of their shoulders, and thus carry it to the great door which opens into the deep veranda of our hospital. Here they leave it, just outside the threshold, and run away and hide themselves, while four of our Christian nurses from the hospital go out and carry the precious burden inside of the veranda, closing the door after them. Here the carriage door is opened, and the occupants are taken out and allowed to rest on the floor of this great veranda until the hour arrives for opening the dispensary. When this load is properly settled the carriage is put outside the door, and other men bring the next carriage in the caravan of camels, and so on, until all the camels have been unloaded and their occupants deposited on our hospital veranda, where they are quite secluded from public gaze, as before intimated, by the broad pillars, close lattice work, and bamboo chicks. Of course the hospital is a purdah or zenana hospital, no men being allowed inside its gates.

At half past nine o'clock A. M. the physician in charge arrives in her carriage, and then the dispensary work begins. Passing through a large folding door in the center of the great front of the hospital, we find ourselves in a large and pleasant consulting room. The ceiling is very lofty, and from its center is suspended a huge *punkah*, which swings from side to side, keeping the sultry air in motion and rendering the room comfortably cool. The members of the hospital staff have arranged themselves in rows on either side of the space between the door and the doctor's table, and bow low in respectful *salaams* as we pass; afterward standing about in their pure white *sarees*, gracefully draped in Indian fashion, respectfully awaiting orders. Parina, the native interpreter, a Christian woman, stands near by, ready to interpret into English any of the many tongues which may be spoken by the various patients who have gathered from all directions. The side door, leading into the outer hall, is opened, and one patient at a time, each taking her turn, passes into the clerk's office, where her name, approximate age, and any particulars which can be gleaned concerning her personal history and illness are recorded. These people never know the date of their birth, but they approximate their age by certain great epochs. This one says, "I was so big," indicating a height of two feet, "at the time of the mutiny," and so on. Having registered, the patients are admitted, in twos and threes, to the consulting room. I shall endeavor to make them known to you, one at a time, as they come into our presence.

A tiny woman, not larger than a child of ten in this country, makes her way slowly from the clerk's office. She is shrouded in her long white purdah garment, which consists of a cap about the shape of a gentleman's smoking or skull cap, pure white, and hand embroidered. Into the lower edge of this cap is gathered a full flounce of unbleached muslin, which falls to the ground, and even trails

about her, being as long in front as behind. Thus
her entire person is wholly concealed from view.
If you separate the thick folds near the rim of the
cap, about where the eyes are supposed to be, you
will find two small holes in the muslin. They are
about one inch long and two thirds of an inch in
width, and are veiled by a close net, something like
mosquito netting, only of coarser texture. Through
these tiny openings the patient is supposed to be
able to see sufficiently to avoid a fall. Of course
one from without cannot see the face nor even the
eyes of the patient through these small and closely-
screened openings. As she comes near our interpreter, with tender persuasion, seeks to remove
this heavy garment; but the little patient is timid
and shrinking, and resists her overtures. At
length, however, she herself slowly gathers the
heavy folds together and raises them a little at a
time, until from underneath she is able to peer
out and look about. She does this to make sure
that there are no boys or men folk in the room.
Later on she is persuaded to allow the nurses to remove this heavy and oppressive garment, and when
this is done she stands before us in her many-
colored pure silk garments, which are so gracefully
adjusted and so artistically arranged, in point of
coloring and in every other detail, as to render her
a beautiful picture to look upon.

So tiny and wan is she, so emaciated and sad of
face, that you judge her to be the patient; but your
mind is presently disabused of this thought, for she

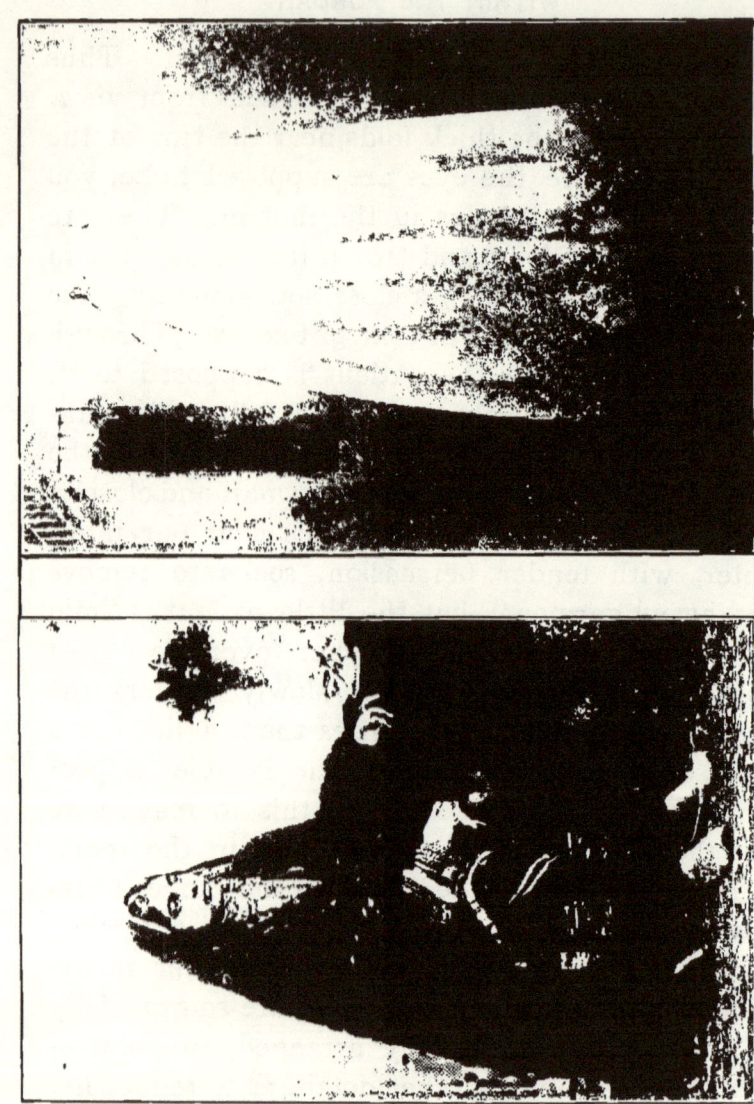

Woman patient in her silk costume of many colors   Woman patient in her long white purdah garment

steps forward and, unwrapping from the folds of her garment an infant, she lays it on the table before you. Its arms and legs are tightly bound down, stiff and straight, by strong strips of cotton cloth. This is the custom throughout the district of Sindh. Be it a boy or a girl, be it Hindu or Mohammedan, all are thus strapped during the first months of their existence; so that the slight exercise, relaxation, and rest which an untrammeled baby naturally gets from tossing its limbs about is denied to infants here. These strips of cloth are tied so tightly about the soft, emaciated limbs that you can almost bury your finger in the groove caused by this pressure. But it is not for this condition we are consulted. The child-mother turns the infant on its side, and you see that the whole back of the head has been crushed until it is quite flat. It is swollen, hot, inflamed, and in the center of the head, at the back, there is a running sore about the size of a silver half-dollar. If you do not know the cause of this condition, your interpreter will explain that every child born of heathen parents in the district of Sindh, boy or girl, Hindu or Mohammedan, is, immediately after birth, placed upon a solid stone bed. Its head rests lower than its trunk, and in order that the child may not slide off headwise and be injured a little ledge is arranged as a headpiece. During the day, every two or three hours, some member of the father-in-law's family, with the strong palm of the hand, presses the soft, mobile little head against this hard stone, until it becomes quite flat at the back, the forehead protrudes, and above each ear large protuberances appear, almost resembling horns. This practice goes on during all the early months of the infant's life, until the head remains in this distorted shape. All this for beauty's sake. These ignorant people imagine that they know better how to form a beautiful human head than does God Almighty. It is the fashion in that part of India, and must be followed—even though the practice result in the death of the child, which is often the case. It seemed to me that every child must die as a result of such treatment. The whole thing was at first incredible to me, and I asked my nurses to call in the servants, and the children of the servants, and uncover their heads, that I might examine them; men's heads in India being always covered with their *pugris*, and the heads of women and girls by their *sarees*. To my astonishment, I found all their heads were perfectly flat at the back and protruding above the ears and in front, as above described.

In the case of this little patient, we will give the infant into the hands of our surgical nurse, asking her to syringe the wound with some disinfectant solution, place a little pillow of surgeon's cotton over and around the wound, bandage the head nicely, as she knows how to do, and bring the child back to us. This done, we restore the little one to its mother's arms, giving strict injunction not again to place it upon its stone bed, and not in any case to remove the bandage, but to bring it back again to-morrow to have the wound dressed. The following day, however, she does not return, nor the next, nor for several weeks. When, however, she does return we discover that the bandages have been removed, and perceive by the condition of the wound that the crushing process has been persisted in, despite the fever which it has caused and the evident debility of the child. We begin to upbraid the little woman. We tell her that she is no mother, that it is a cruel, unnatural thing for her thus to torture her little one, that she has no love for her babe. At these words the tiny mother, with a gesture expressive of utter helplessness and a look of entreaty, exclaims: "O, Doctor Sahiba, what can I do? It is our custom! And then," she adds, in a still more helpless way, " I have a cruel mother-in-law." So it is that, though the child-mother might perhaps spare her infant this torture, there are other members of the family who would insist upon carrying out the custom of their people. Of course the little head is dressed again as before, and the patient and mother sent away with stronger orders than ever; but she never again returns—not at least for the sake of this child. Some months later she does come back to consult us in regard to an older child, and when we interrogate her concerning her baby she tells us in a sad way that it is dead.

The practices above described, of binding the limbs and crushing the heads of infants born to heathen parents residing in the district or province

3

of Sindh, are, as has already been intimated, inflicted upon both male and female children, but if
the little one is so unfortunate as to be born a girl
in this district, there are many tortures which she
must endure from which her brother would be
exempt.

Our next patient is also an infant in the arms of
her young mother. Upon examination we find the
little limbs tightly banded down and the head
crushed, as in the former instance, but in addition
to this the wee ears have been pierced every eighth
of an inch all around the rims, and dirty-looking,
black woolen strings have been inserted in the
freshly-wounded tender flesh. The nose, also, both
right and left nostrils and the center portion, has
been pierced, and the woolen strings have so irri-
tated the wounds that both the nose and the ears
have become enormously swollen, hot, and ulcer-
ated to such an extent as to render the child
feverish and ill. These running sores—shall I say
it to refined ears?—are full of maggots, which add a
fresh torture to the sufferings already too great. If
we are new in Sindh, and have not yet learned how
utterly useless it is to fight against these iron-clad
customs, we will probably follow our first impera-
tive impulse—clip the strings and remove them
from the ears and nostrils; afterward passing the
child to the nurse with instructions to syringe with
disinfectant solution and dress the wounds properly.
This done, we give instructions to the mother to
allow the bandages to remain and to bring back the

child to the dispensary to-morrow. The mother does not return with the child for many days. When, finally, she does return she approaches timidly and with apparent shamefacedness. She does not carry her infant, but her mother-in-law follows on behind with the babe in her arms, while the little mother comes toward us, bowing at every step until her forehead almost touches the floor. This formality indicates that she acknowledges her own great inferiority, that she feels herself to be little and mean and contemptible—less than the dust under your feet, a very slave; while you, in her own words, are her *ma bap* (mother and father), great, and high, and lifted up, with authority to command or crush her at your pleasure; nevertheless she comes to you with a petition. As she draws near we will await her further formality.

Standing before us, she takes the corner of her *sarce*, wraps it around her neck, and holds it tightly with her two hands. This to us, suggests hanging, and it is a sort of mental hanging, for it means exactly the same as the low *salaam* above described. Standing now with bowed head, and joining the tips of index fingers, she begins to stroke the bridge of her nose. This formality, also, has the same significance as the two preceding ones. Finally you grow impatient, and express your willingness to hear her petition at once. The mother-in-law now comes forward and lays the infant on the table before you. The bandages have been removed from the head, black strings have again been inserted, and the child is in a worse condition, if possible, than on the occasion of the first visit. The little mother now interposes and begs that you do not again remove the strings from her baby's ears, but that you give some lotion or ointment which can be applied, and which will cause the wounds to heal, while the strings remain in their places; adding, with all the emphasis which she is capable of expressing, that, if you remove them, she cannot again bring the child to the dispensary, because her family will have other strings inserted immediately upon her return. The strings, she declares, must remain, because her little girl is soon to be married, and then ornaments will be inserted in place of the strings. The native Indian has a conviction that the English ointment is an infallible cure-all. No matter what the disease, no matter how terrible the condition, if an Indian can procure a little English ointment, a perfect cure is certain. In this case, if we are wise—if we have been in this part of India for long, and understand how perfectly impossible it is to overthrow the customs of these people and how futile all efforts to prevent the carrying out of them—we will accede to the petition of the little mother. We will not again cut the strings from the baby's ears and nostrils, but we will have the wounds syringed with a disinfectant solution and give her some lotion or powder or ointment, to apply from time to time, which will facilitate the healing of the wounds, even while the strings remain. By these means

we shall be able at least to relieve the sufferings of
our little patient, though we cannot wholly remove
them; whereas, if we were to cut the strings, the
mother would never again return to the dispensary
with her child, and it would be allowed to suffer on
without relief.

If this little girl baby is so unfortunate, as we
would consider her—so fortunate, as the natives of
India would consider—as to have an elder brother,
she will be left upon her stone bed from morning
until evening, and from evening until morning.
She will be fed upon goat's milk if her parents are
wealthy; if poor, rice, *chapati*, or any food that it
is convenient to give. If she cry, and thus annoy
the family, she will be dosed with opium, while her
brother—two, three, four, five, or six years of age,
perhaps a large boy nearly as tall as his mother—
will sit astride his mother's hip and receive from
her the natural nourishment which God Almighty
provided for the young infant. Whatever the
mother is doing, however laborious her task, she
can never be rid of this great, strong child, which
hangs continually upon her side. If she put him
down for a moment, he will kick and scream,
tear her hair, scratch and bite her until she is
obliged to take him again upon her thigh. She
dare not strike him or punish him in any way, for
he is her husband's son. If you question her as to
this strange partiality between her two children, she
will reply, " O, the baby is only a girl, but *this*—
my *son!* "

You will naturally judge from this that Indian parents love their sons and hate their daughters. I believe this, also, to be a mistake. Where there is any love it is felt just as much for the daughter as for the son. I have seen this exemplified in many cases. I remember one instance in which the little daughter had fallen from an upstairs veranda and received fatal injuries. The mother told us about it with many tears, and my interpreter said to her: "What does it matter? She was only a girl!" The mother replied, "Yes, she was only a girl; but then what about my mother-heart?" The fact is that where you find heathen people who know nothing about Christ, nothing about the one great God whose name is Love, nothing about his revealed truth, which teaches love, there is very little love to be found; and this difference in the treatment of the daughter and son comes through no partiality for the son, on his own account, but from a purely business and mercenary principle. The son, from the day of his birth to the day of his burial or burning (for, if he be a Mohammedan, his remains will be buried; if a Hindu, they will be burned), is a source of great honor and large income to his parents. Indeed, among these people the birth of a son is considered to be well-nigh equivalent to receiving a fortune; whereas the daughter, from the day of her birth to the day of her burial or burning, is not only a source of tremendous expense—an expense which never ceases while she lives—but she is also a source of possible disgrace

to her family and caste. If she be not married
before she arrive at the age of twelve, she can never
marry, as no native man will marry a girl over that
age, and her parents and all their family are irreparably disgraced. Indeed, nothing can happen to
a native family which will bring them such disgrace
as this. The parents are supposed to have failed
in their duty to their child. A girl thus unmarried
is in a worse condition than a widow. She is
stripped of her jewels and silken apparel; a single
scant garment of coarse texture is all that is allowed
to her, and her beautiful hair is cut. She is not allowed to mingle with the other members of the
family during any festivity or anniversary occasion.
If there be rejoicings in the home at the birth or
marriage of a son, or on account of any other good
fortune, she may not participate in it. She must
sit alone in a little dark place nursing her miseries,
and never showing her face to mother, father,
brother, sister, or guest. Even on ordinary occasions she may not show her face in the morning to
any member of the family until they have each and
all looked into other faces of happier fortune; for
she is supposed to be cursed by the gods, and for
one to behold her face before seeing the faces of
others would, in the opinion of natives, invariably
bring bad luck. She does the drudgery of her
father's household, and receives kicks and abuses
from any and all of its members, and often upon
the slightest provocation. Should she fall ill, no
physician is consulted and no effort made to restore

her health or to prolong her life. Her death is earnestly hoped for not only by her family and friends, but by herself also. .

On one occasion a native zenana worker who taught one of the respectable married sisters of one of these little unfortunate unmarried girls begged the father to allow her to bring a physician, not with any hope of restoring health, or even prolonging life, but simply with the object of relieving the intense suffering which this daughter, who was far gone in consumption, was so patiently enduring. On several occasions the zenana worker had begged permission to do this, but the father was not willing to pay any medical fees, and still less willing to have the health of his daughter restored or her life prolonged. Finally, however, she obtained permission to bring a lady physician, with the understanding that no fees should be charged and no effort made to restore the health or prolong the life of the patient, but only to relieve the pain. The native zenana worker then explained the case to me, and I readily agreed to the terms, consenting to pay the visit without charge and with the sole object of relieving the most distressing symptoms. I can never forget my visit. The expression of utter hopelessness, despair, and misery on this young girl's face beggars description. The memory of it haunted me for many days afterward. During a subsequent visit, and through my interpreter, I carefully described to my little patient God's great plan of salvation. I assured her that she was immortal—that she could never die. I said, "The part of you that thinks, that feels, that suffers, that rejoices, that understands—that part must live forever, and forever, and forever." I told her Christ would prepare a place for her in heaven, and that he would take her to himself if she would only believe on him and give her heart to him. She listened with intense eagerness, her eyes dilating, her face flushing and then growing pale again. She had been taught to believe that she had no soul, being a woman, and that her only hope would have been in marriage, which the gods had denied her. A married woman may hope, by the faithful discharge of her duties to her husband, obedience to her mother-in-law, etc., etc., some time to be born again in the form of a man, and after that, perhaps, she may merge into the great God, and thus lose her individuality and identity; but a woman who has been cursed of the gods, and for whom a husband could not be found, has no hope in this life or in the next. When, however, she heard the true story of the creation, the fall, the redemption of the world through the death of Christ, the immortality of the soul, and God's great plan of salvation, she accepted it with the simplicity of a young child, and, trusting in the Lord Jesus Christ for her eternal salvation, she received him into her heart gladly, joyfully. How can I tell it? No words can describe the wonderful change which swept over her pale, sad face. If she had ever known joy, if there had ever been a ray of hope in her heart, it had left no trace upon her poor, wan countenance. Now, for the first time, her face was lighted up with joy and hope and peace; and in her large dark eyes a wonderful love-light came, and remained until all light was gone and her spirit was with God.

As soon as a female child is born in any household the preparations for rejoicing, which had been made in anticipation of a son, are put aside, and no one is allowed to partake of food in that house for some time thereafter, as there is now cause for sadness and not rejoicing. The father begins immediately to cast about in his mind for some one to whom he may betroth his new-born daughter. This is arranged as quickly as possible. He will betroth her to an infant boy if convenient, or to a boy in his childhood, or in his youth, or in his young manhood; or to a man in middle life, or even to an old man with many wives. The only imperatively necessary thing is that she be betrothed to some boy or man in her own caste, and that without delay. Of course, in any case, the bridegroom may die before the wee girl is yet old enough to be married, and thus she will be left a widow. This, however, would not be so dire a catastrophe as for her to remain unmarried until she pass the age of twelve. In the former case she only is disgraced, and is supposed to have incurred the curse of the gods; whereas in the latter case her parents and all their family are disgraced, deeply and irreparably, among all their caste people.

The betrothal involves much expense to the little

Wealthy Hindu Bridegroom and his Child-Bride

girl's father. He is expected to make a feast for
the bridegroom's family and friends. To the future
bridegroom's father, mother, brothers, and sisters
he is expected to give *bakhshish* (gifts). We hear a
great *tamashi* (noise, sound of rejoicing) in the
street, and, rushing to the door, we see a horse, if
the family are in good circumstances, otherwise a
bullock, donkey, or goat, adorned with wreaths of
flowers, gold and silver trappings, and carrying
upon his back the bridegroom, who is also adorned
with gold, silver, and flowers in the most striking
manner. If his parents be wealthy, he may also be
adorned with jewels of many sorts and colors.
Men and boys crowd about, and there is a sound of
beating of drums, cymbals, and various musical instruments of native device. Somewhere behind in
the crowd there is a bullock cart, closely curtained
on all sides, and in this purdah-carriage is the baby
girl whose betrothal is now being celebrated. Of
course it may be that she has arrived at the age of
one, two, three, four, or five years, and that her
parents have been unable to arrange for this betrothal earlier; but whether she be an infant of a
few days only or a little girl of five or six years,
she will be closely concealed in the purdah-carriage,
accompanied by her mother or nurse, or both, neither of whom can be seen by the people who
throng the carriage. After this ceremony the wedding day must not too long be postponed. "How
long?" do you ask? A few years ago the English
government passed a law to the effect that no bride

should go to the house of her mother-in-law before she arrived at the age of twelve years. I am a witness, however, as is every practicing physician in India, that this law is utterly ignored. Of course a law is useless unless it is enforced; but who can enforce such a law as this? Who knows the age of the little girl-wife when she goes from her mother's home to the house of her mother-in-law? She is a zenana woman. No European, no man, except her nearest relatives, has ever seen her form or face. No one knows her age except her nearest relatives, and they all acquiesce in the practice of child-marriage. Should the English authorities suspect the true age of this little bride to be less than that required by the law, and prosecute the parents, the father of the child would take his affidavit unhesitatingly to the effect that she has passed the age of twelve, even though she were really only six, seven, or eight years of age. Often and often have I treated little women patients of five, six, seven, eight, and nine years, who were at that time living with their husbands, and came to our dispensary accompanied by their mother-in-law, which is in itself a proof of the fact.

The wedding ceremony involves the father of the bride in many additional and very heavy expenses. He must again give a dinner to the bridegroom's family and friends; he must again give gifts to every member of that household. He must purchase for his daughter many gold and silver ornaments. Her ears must have gold and

silver rings all around, every eighth of an inch.
She must wear necklaces that begin tightly about
the neck, increasing in length until they well-nigh
cover her chest and reach down to her waist. Her
fingers must have rings upon them, and her toes
must have rings also. The latter must be solid
silver, with blue enamel on the diamond-shaped
tops, in the center of which there is a little hook
holding a tiny silver bell, which renders the little
woman incapable of moving without starting the
jingle of silver. It is said that this custom was
invented in order that the mother-in-law might
know the exact whereabouts of her daughter-in-
law. Upon her ankles she wears heavy silver
anklets, so heavy and angular in shape as to soon
cause the slight ankle to become quite callous all
around. Through her left nostril she wears a gold
ring of small size. In the septum there is also a
gold ring, to which is attached a long pendant,
which droops over the mouth, and requires to be
lifted whenever she eats or drinks. The wedding ring must be of pure gold, made in the shape
of a bugle, the most slender part of which passes
through the right nostril. It is always very large,
often interfering with the sight of the right eye.
If the parents are poor, the wedding ring may be
hollow; but if they are wealthy, it must be solid, in
which case it is very heavy. Indeed, any of them
are sufficiently heavy to tear out the nostril, so that
it is a common thing at our dispensary to repair noses
thus rent; although this ring is usually supported

in part by a braid of hair brought from the back of the head down over the forehead and along the bridge of the nose. Her arms are covered with tight ivory bangles, extending from the wrist close down to the hand and up to the bend of the elbow. At this point a small space is left, to allow flexion and extension of the joint. Just above the elbow the bangles begin again, extending to the shoulder. The bangles are made to fit the arm so tightly as to badly callous the wrist and, what is worse, to interfere with the circulation of the blood, so that the hands become swollen, purple, and very painful, while the uncovered space at the elbow joint swells enormously, often forming abscesses which require to be lanced. These abscesses are intensely painful, and yet the mother-in-law will on no consideration allow even two or three of the bangles to be removed in order to relieve this terrible suffering. They (the bangles) are a sign of the child's respectable married condition, and to remove them would be a disgrace, indicating her widowhood. Indeed, they can never be removed during her life, unless her husband first die. Now, if you remember that on her wedding day she is a mere child, you will know that she must grow, and is almost sure at one time or another to take on some additional flesh, and in either case the pain recurs, abscesses forming again and again. However large she may become, these bangles, which have cost her father the considerable sum of eighty or ninety rupees, are never exchanged for a larger size. When they are first placed upon her arms they render her almost helpless for a week or more; she is unable to feed herself, to dress her hair, or to make her own toilet; so that a friend must wait upon her until the tender flesh shrinks away from this firm, unyielding pressure, and she becomes accustomed to the stiffness, and is thus able to resume her daily duties.

These, however, are not the only nor the greater of the many expenses which the father is expected to meet on the day of his daughter's marriage. He must pay into the hands of his daughter's father-in-law the, to him, great sum of two thousand rupees. His income does not, in all probability, exceed five dollars a month, and with this he must support his family, which is probably large. In order to raise the two thousand rupees at one time he will need to mortgage the ornaments of his wife, his daughters-in-law, if he be so fortunate as to have any, and perhaps his brothers and other near relatives will need to do the same in order to enable him to raise the required amount. To liquidate this debt and to redeem the ornaments mortgaged will probably require the remainder of his life—unless he be so fortunate as to have a son or two who may marry and thus get back the two thousand rupees, together with ornaments, and secure a daughter-in-law who will serve as family drudge and slave. Nor does the father's expense cease when he has his daughter safely married and sent to the home of her mother-in-law. If she fall ill at any time, it becomes his duty and the duty of his wife to pay her regular visits at stated intervals, and on every such occasion his wife must pay into the hand of this daughter's mother-in-law a sum of money not less than eight annas. Should the parents not visit their daughter when ill, or should they visit her seldom, they will be considered by their caste people to have failed in their parental duty, and will be in disgrace as a result.

On the other hand, the son is a source of income and honor to his parents as long as he lives. He may be betrothed at any time after his birth; and this, as shown above, brings a feast and gifts to his father's family. Later on he is married, which means two thousand rupees—a small fortune—to his father. Besides this, all the jewels with which the little wife is adorned may be mortgaged or sold by her father-in-law, as they are all of pure gold or silver. Moreover, the little daughter-in-law actually serves in her father-in-law's house as a family drudge and the slave of her mother-in-law. This is the only hope of the Indian woman. If she be blessed with a son, she looks forward to the time when he will marry and her labors cease, and when she will be respected and envied by all the native women because she has a married son and a daughter-in-law to serve her. Moreover, this same son may be married several times, even if his wives all live; or if one or more of them die, it affords him still greater opportunity for marrying, and each new wife will bring to his father a small fortune. Besides all this, he must of necessity follow the occupation of his father, and early in his life he may begin to earn a regular salary, which in every case he passes over to his father, who is the head of the house as long as he lives. Thus a son in India is a source of increasing wealth and respectability to his parents, while the daughter is the reverse.

To return to our dispensary. We find several little women waiting to have their ears repaired; for not only does the nose ring tear out the nostril, but it is a more common occurrence to have the ears torn through. The earrings worn in this part of the country by the poor and middle classes are solid silver rings of immense size, and covered with great, sharp protuberances. These rings pull the upper half of the ear down over the lower half until the whole ear is stretched and distorted so that you would scarcely recognize it. Thus the great silver rings are piled one upon another; being inserted, as has already been stated, every eighth of an inch all the way around the rim of the ear, and standing out from the head two or three inches like great horns. Whenever one of these rings tears its way through the ear, so that it drops to the floor, the mother-in-law will immediately pierce another hole and put the ring back in its place; and this she will do as long as there is any space left. When, finally, there is no longer any sound part through which a hole can be bored in the little woman's ear, when the entire rim of that delicate organ is

4

slitted and slashed like the ragged edge of a frayed
garment, then the mother-in-law will bring her to
the hospital to have her ears repaired. Not that
she cares in the least for the disfiguration thus
caused or for the deformity; that is a matter of no
consequence. The chief object of lading the wife
with ornaments and jewels is not that she may be
adorned, that her beauty may be enhanced—it is a
business arrangement. The wife is the bank of
her husband. He is distrustful of Englishmen and
of English banks; he fears to bury his gold in the
earth, lest its hiding place be discovered by robbers;
but his wife is in purdah, kept in close seclusion;
no robber can get at her without great difficulty.
He therefore invests every spare rupee in a solid
gold or silver ornament to be hung upon his wife's
person. This can be mortgaged or sold at any
time, and is just so much cash to him. They are
not careful that the gold and silver ornaments be
beautifully molded or carved. It is a common
thing to see a very rough gold nugget made into a
necklace, the several parts of which are beaten
out in the crudest manner. The natives of India
object to anæsthetics, and think it quite unnecessary to administer anything for the, to them,
trifling operation of repairing such rents. It is an
everyday occurrence to have several such patients
at our dispensary, and to see one after another sit
down quietly and have two, three, or more rents in
each ear denuded and sewed up, and one or two
such in the right nostril. During the whole opera-

tion, which is really a very painful one, the little
patient will never wince, nor cry out, nor make any
sign of pain. She is so inured to suffering that this
is easily borne.

Here comes another patient from the clerk's
office. She resembles the others in size, but seems
to be rather older than the first-mentioned, though
still young. She is very lame, and walks with
difficulty. Her mother-in-law precedes her; a
young native woman is never permitted to leave
her husband's house except she is accompanied by
her mother-in-law. Presently they stand before
us, and the mother-in-law begins to explain that
her daughter-in-law is a very bad, ill-tempered,
naughty child, and that recently, in a fit of temper,
she threw herself from the roof of the house and
lamed herself badly. We turn to the little patient
for her version of the story. She repeats almost
precisely the words just spoken by her mother-in-
law. She confesses herself to be very ill-tempered
and naughty, and declares that she injured herself
in leaping from the roof of the house. After
making a careful examination of my patient I am
convinced that both mother-in-law and daughter-
in-law have lied; and so I determine, for once in
their lives, to separate this mother-in-law from her
daughter-in-law. Bidding the former remain
where she is, I take the little wife into my private
consulting room, and the door is fastened; then I
bring a chair and persuade the little woman to sit
down upon it. This she is very loath to do, as she

has never been allowed to sit in the presence of any person whom she respects. Finally, however, she takes the chair by my side. I now assure her that I am her friend. I tell her about my happy home in America; that I have a father who loves me and brothers who love me and are kind to me, but that I heard of her; I knew her life was unhappy, that her friends were not gentle and kind to her as mine were to me, and because of my love for the dear Lord, who came to earth to suffer and to die for her and for me, I left my home in the far-off land, and came across the waters, away over to India, in order that I might somehow *help her*. I ask her if she believes all this; if she believes that I am her friend; but long before I have reached this point the little woman is convulsed with sobs. Indian women, especially in Sindh, seldom weep on account of harsh words, unkindness, or pain of any sort, however severe. They are inured to suffering; but when you declare yourself to be their friend, when you speak to them kind, tender words, it is not difficult to find their hearts. And so, as soon as she is able to speak, she confesses that she believes me to be her friend; that she never had a friend or anyone to love her, and that no one ever talked to her thus before in all her life. In reply I tell her I am her physician; that I wish to make her well and strong, but cannot do so unless I know the facts of her case. I tell her that I am fully aware that both she and her mother-in-law misrepresented the case to me in the general consulting room. I know from the character of her wounds that she never got them by jumping from the roof of a house. "So now," I say, "won't you tell me the truth? Won't you tell me just how you got these wounds and bruises? I shall not tell your mother-in-law. I shall not tell any of your caste people, but I want to know all about it; the whole truth." She promises to tell me the truth, and then begins by saying that she is a very naughty girl and very ill-tempered. I stop her and remind her of her promise to tell me the truth. She assures me again that she will tell me the truth. She fully believes this to be true. She has been told all her life that she was the worst and most ill-tempered creature on the face of the earth, and she has no doubt of its truth; and so she begins again with the same confession, after which she proceeds to say that on one occasion a brother-in-law asked her to do something which she felt herself really too weak to do. She was so tired, so weak, and so hungry that she did not instantly obey his command, perhaps she even answered back, whereupon he felled her to the earth. Another came along and kicked her, and still another member of her husband's family beat her with a club until she became unconscious. She does not know what happened after that, but she imagines they thought they had killed her, and were frightened on account of the English government; at any rate, after she came to herself she found they had dragged her behind the house, in the narrow space between it and the great wall which surrounds it. When she raised her head and looked about she saw her mother-in-law peeping around the corner. As soon as she was able she dragged herself out where she could get a drink of water. All this happened two weeks ago. Since then she has been gradually improving, but has not yet been able to work much, and because of this latter her mother-in-law, judging her to be so far recovered that the doctor at the hospital would believe her story about leaping from the roof of the house, determined to bring her to the dispensary in order that she might be made well enough to work.

This is one case only; many such have I treated in Hyderabad. Little frail creatures come into the hospital all black and blue, and maimed from head to foot, from brutal kicks and club beatings which they have received at the hands of mother-in-law, brothers-in-law, sisters-in-law, and other members of the husband's household; and this often upon the slightest provocation. Do you question why the English government permits such outrages? It is plain enough. The English government does not and would not permit it if the English government had any power to prevent it.

Suppose that I, as an English government physician, in charge of this dispensary, were to prosecute the perpetrators of this outrage. A day would be appointed for the hearing. The case must needs be tried in a small-cause court, as all such cases

come under this head, and these courts are all
presided over by native judges. On the day of
hearing the father-in-law, his sons, brothers, and
other relatives, together with perhaps fifty or more
outside witnesses (who for two annas each are
willing to swear to anything), all give evidence to
the same effect; that, from such, or such, or such a
distance, he saw this little woman leap from the
roof of her father-in-law's house and had personally
heard her cries, knowing that she must have been
injured by the fall. They would each and all
testify to the perfectly upright, honorable, and respectable character of the father-in-law's family.
After such overwhelming evidence as this, all
coming from eyewitnesses (?), what weight would
my evidence have? I testify that on a certain
occasion, in my private consulting room, this
little child-wife gave a very different explanation
as to the cause of her wounds. Perhaps my interpreter is also present, and confirms my evidence. To overbalance this, however, the little
child-wife herself, in her close purdah garment, is
brought into court, and there takes her affidavit
that she leaped from the roof of her father-in-law's
house in a fit of anger, and thus wounded herself.
She will perhaps also testify that she is very ill-
tempered and bad, and that her husband's family
are all very good and kind to her. She dare not, for
her life, testify otherwise. Of course the judge will
dismiss the case. It may be that away down in his
heart he is convinced that the little American doc-

tor somehow must have gotten a confession of the truth from this little Indian woman, but he is, nevertheless, glad that she has not sufficient evidence to prove the facts in the case. For he himself would treat his own daughter-in-law in like manner; indeed, he considers that the husband or father-in-law has a perfect right to take the life of his wife or daughter-in-law if he feels so inclined.

As already intimated, the daughter-in-law is a drudge and slave in her husband's home. Early in the morning, before any other members of the family are awake, she is up; and sitting in front of the door on the ground, she grinds the wheat for the day's consumption. The wheat is ground between two great stones, the upper one having a hole in its center, through which the wheat falls from the hand of the grinder. The upper stone has also a wooden handle at one side by which it is turned around and around. This is the same sort of a mill as that referred to in the Bible: "Two women shall be grinding at the mill." If there are two daughters-in-law in the family, the two will share this labor, one sitting on either side of the mill. They are supposed to sing a grinding song while engaged in this task, and for the song to cease before the wheat is ground would be sufficient offense to justify a blow from any member of the husband's family. This is very arduous labor, and the slight little women sometimes faint away while engaged in the task. Later in the day the *degchas* (brass and copper cooking utensils) must be scoured

A Little Daughter-in-law Scouring the Degchas

with the palm of the hand until they shine like mirrors. Common soil from the front of the door is used for this purpose.

In this part of India the fashion allows the daughter-in-law, in the early, early morning, before anyone else is astir, to break her fast with any cold food, rice curry or *chapati* (pancake, made of flour and water), which may have been left over from the day before. If there chance to be no such cold food in the house, which is often the case, then her fast must remain unbroken during the long hours of that hot, sultry day. Though she prepare all the food for the family, no particle may pass her lips. She prepares the food and stands serving while the others eat, but she has nothing to satisfy her own hunger until late at night, nine or ten o'clock, when all the family have eaten, smoked the *huqqa* (native pipe), gossiped, and retired to rest; then, if there be cold food left in the house, any which has not been consumed during the day, she may take of this to satisfy her hunger. Consequently—a natural result of this custom—the mother-in-law is often obliged to bring her little half-starved daughter-in-law to the dispensary for treatment. She will then stand before you and declare that the girl-wife is very lazy; that she does not love work; and that often while engaged in grinding her wheat, or some other domestic task, she pretends a faint and seems to become unconscious. She assures you that this cannot be real; she is certain that the child is only shirking work, but adds that, though she beat her, she will not resume her task; and when, finally, she returns to consciousness and goes back to her work she will perhaps faint again. She then instructs you that in case you find any serious disease upon the child which is likely to be fatal it is a matter of no consequence. She does not care to prolong her life if she is likely to die, for she is only a girl, and no good on earth. But if she live, she must work; so, if you do not find anything serious the matter with her, she will be glad to have you give her something that will make her strong to work. During all this harangue the daughter-in-law's face does not alter in its expression. She has heard such talk as this all her life, and she cannot be more grieved than she has ever been. The same look of settled, helpless despondency remains on her countenance. We examine the frail little patient. Her body is emaciated almost to a skeleton; her little pulse flutters and intermits. We find no organic disease present, and we know by many signs that she is in a condition of chronic starvation. We interrogate the mother-in-law as to her food—when she eats, what she eats, how often she takes food, and in what quantities. Unblushingly the mother-in-law refers to the above custom, which allows the daughter-in-law to eat the remnants of food which are left over from the family meals during the early morning hour and late at night. We tell her that she is starving the child to death; and ask her if she will not provide at least

one cup of milk every day at noon, or one egg; or
at least make sure that the child does get something to eat in the middle of the day regularly.
In answer the mother-in-law straightens herself
up, and with a sarcastic smile she assures you
that that child's small stomach is not able to contain
more food than she gets. By this you know that,
while for the sake of the work she is willing to
bring her daughter-in-law to the dispensary to get
medicine which costs her nothing, she will not go
to the expense of one extra *pie* (a small copper coin,
worth about one sixth of a cent) for the sake of improving her daughter-in-law's health or prolonging
her life. We have a secret closet in our hospital,
of which I carry the key. It contains beef extract,
mutton extract, essence of chicken, soups, and other
nourishing preparations. "My Esther," my Christian
matron, and one or two of my Christian nurses
know about this closet, and so I give to one of them
the key, and she understands what is meant. Presently she returns with a large bottle, having upon it
a very imposing scarlet label, directing that the
patient take one wineglassful of the contents every
hour. Of course, if these high-caste natives knew
that I was feeding a member of their family upon
beef or mutton, or any other meat preparation, my
life would no longer be safe in their midst. They
do not know it, however, and there is little danger
of their ever finding it out, as none of them would
know the taste of meat, however prepared, if they
were fed upon it. By this means we are able at

least to prevent the child from starvation, and to give her a little strength whereby she may perform her daily task without excessive fatigue.

I have endeavored to describe a few of my most interesting patients in order to acquaint you with those peculiar pathological conditions which result from the strange and cruel practices of this most barbarous people. I have not mentioned any of the many cases of leprosy which come to our dispensary for treatment; nor yet that even more loathsome but unnamable disease which prevails to such an alarming extent throughout this part of India; nor smallpox, which is sometimes seen; nor cholera, many cases of which we have during every cholera season. It has not been my object to discuss medical subjects, nor to outline the treatment of diseases peculiar to India; but rather merely to touch upon those self-inflicted tortures which acquaint us with the cruel customs, prejudices, and barbarous practices of these people in their inner home-life. Perhaps, if you were there with me in person, instead of being there merely in imagination, the thing which would leave the deepest and the most indelible impression upon your mind, more than any diseased condition which I have named or could name, is the expression upon the countenances of these women—old and young. As we enter together the great front door which leads into the front veranda, and you cast your eyes over the crowd of women and children that sit upon the floor of that veranda, you will see upon their faces an expression of settled, unchanging, hopeless misery, which it is utterly impossible to describe. The children are not playing around with one another. There seems to be no real child-life among them; it has been utterly crushed out; unless, indeed, there happen to be some little boys in the crowd. The girls, though little more than babes, sit quietly on the floor, like old women, wearing the same look of hopeless despair and wretchedness. You never see these little girls at play; you never see a happy, joyous expression upon their countenances. And many women at the age of thirty appear to be decrepit, worn-out, old women.

My work in the hospital at Hyderabad was delightful. There was nothing difficult or arduous in connection with it. I had a full staff of efficient hospital assistants, who seemed to vie with each other in rendering me the most prompt, efficient, anticipative service. My work was only the purely medical and surgical. Indeed, much of the medical and surgical work I could safely intrust to either "My Esther," my matron, or my head nurse. The hospital records were prepared by the hospital clerk; I had only to review, correct, and sign them. Even my prescriptions were written by another at my dictation. My compounder, or druggist, never made a mistake in the putting up of his medicines or in the labeling of them. Only the examination, diagnosis, and prescribing for my medical patients and the performing of major operations devolved upon me; and, of course, the overseeing and managing of the whole. All this was pure delight to me, as I love medicine and surgery and everything in connection with it; and yet, I assure you, often and often I have returned home from my dispensary and thrown myself upon my face in utter weariness of body and mind—not because of any work which I had performed, but simply on account of the heartrending stories of suffering to which I had listened and the horrible conditions which I had witnessed, but which I felt myself so utterly helpless to materially better. Indeed, I often questioned in my mind whether there could be any real advantage in relieving the present merely physical suffering, and prolonging human life in cases where the heart, the mind, the soul, writhed in agony, being so much more hopelessly diseased—the heart sufferings exceeding in such great measure any possibility of physical pain.

Will you go with me to visit one out-patient? The messenger is a Hindu prince. He comes in a fine English phaeton, drawn by four horses. He has two coachmen on the box, two standing behind. He himself is attired in pure white garments, with the peculiar tall silk hat, with its crown downward and its rim above, which is worn by every wealthy and distinguished native gentleman in the district of Sindh. He is a man of sixty or sixty-five years of age, and his hair is quite white. He informs me that one of his wives is very ill, and that he wishes me to go at once to see her. I take my seat in the carriage, with "My Esther" at my side. We pass

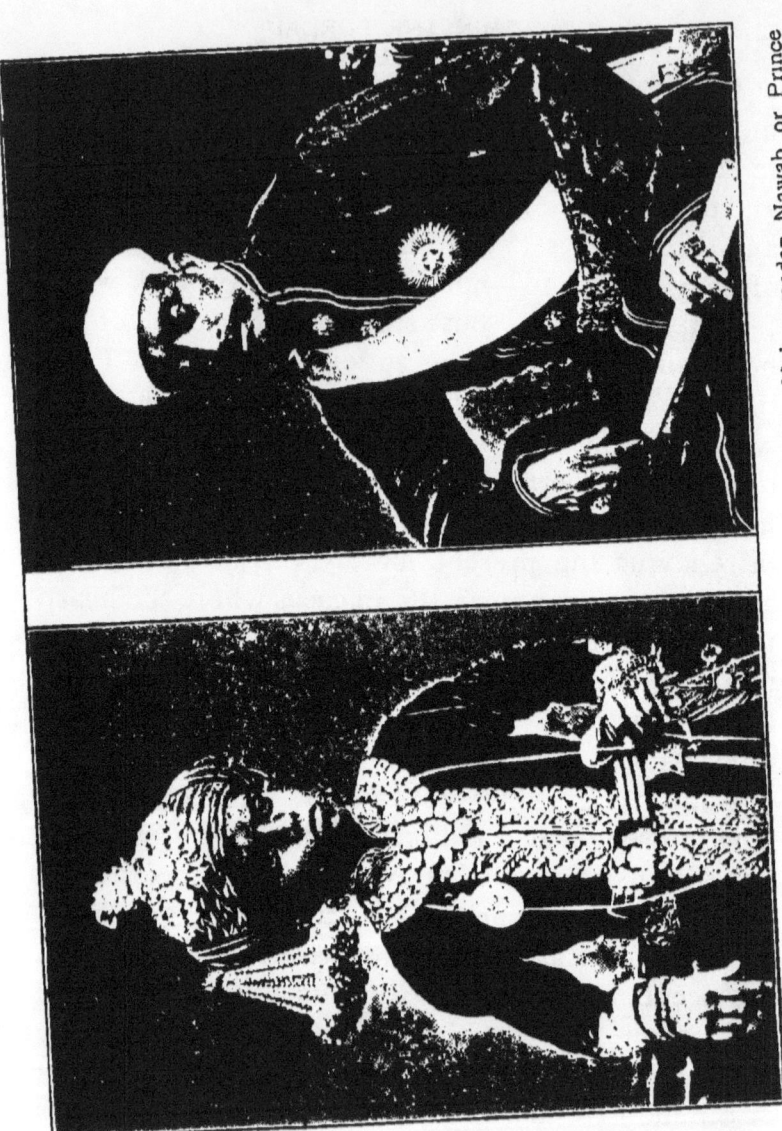

A Wealthy Mohammedan Nawab, or Prince

A Young Hindu Prince

through the narrow streets of the native city until we reach a great gateway opening through a tall wall which surrounds the premises. At this gate we alight from our carriage and, passing through a very small gate in the center of one of the two doors of which the large gate is composed, we find ourselves in the courtyard of the prince. This court is about thirty by sixty feet in size, and is surrounded by a great wall. At the farther end you see a deep veranda with a sloping roof, which obstructs the skylight so much as to render it quite dark. We cross the courtyard and enter the veranda, from which we pass through a large folding door into the one apartment which constitutes the home of this prince. It is a room of about fifteen by thirty feet in size. There is no window in the room, nor any opening except the door through which we entered. The apartment has a ground floor. You see no furniture about, but the place is crowded with women and children of all ages. As soon as our eyes become accustomed to the dimness we are conducted to a corner of the room behind the door, where, stretched upon the floor, we find the emaciated form of a woman of about thirteen or fourteen years of age. She is the fourth wife of the prince, though there is such a remarkable discrepancy in their ages. I get down on the ground floor by the side of my little patient, in order to examine her carefully. I find no organic disease, but soon perceive that she is starving to death. I prescribe one of the large bottles from the secret

closet in my dispensary, and volunteer to supply a
trained nurse, without charge, in order that my little patient may have every attention and may be
sure to get the medicine and the other nourish-
ments which I prescribe at regular intervals. The
prince, however, gladly accepting the medicine, not
knowing its ingredients, refuses the services of my
nurse, assuring me that his wife shall have every
attention and that my minutest orders shall be
scrupulously carried out. Thus we leave them.
The following day the same carriage stops again in
front of my bungalow door. The prince has come
to take me again to his home. As we drive along
through the streets of the native city he tells me
that his wife, my patient, is a very troublesome little woman, and that she has refused to take my
medicine and the nourishment which I prescribed.
He assures me that she holds me in great reverence,
and that if I but exercise my authority over her,
scold her a little and command her sternly, she
will obey me and there will be no further trouble.
Again in the dark corner with my patient, I request
"My Esther" to clear the room, which is crowded
with women and children as before. This is no easy
task. With arms extended, as if she were driving
a flock of geese, and with many words she attempts
to get the women and children into the courtyard.
At my request the prince assists in this process of
driving; but as fast as they are gotten out of the
door they slip back again, stooping under the out-
stretched arms of "My Esther," and crowding back

"My Esther," Mrs. Mary Esther Isaac Ilahi Baksh

into some dark corner where they may see and hear all that is going on. At length, however, the room is empty, and I request the lord of the place to stand in the door and guard the way, that no person may enter again. This I do with the double motive of keeping the women and children out and meantime keeping him away also. Of course I cannot close the door, for all the light we get comes through it, and the room would be perfectly dark if the door were closed. Sitting down on the ground by the side of my patient, I take her little emaciated hand between my two large palms, and with low-pitched voice I begin talking to her very much in the same way as I talked to the little girl who had been beaten. I tell her about my home in America, my family and friends there; I tell her about the Lord Jesus Christ and his love for her and for me; how he left his home in heaven to come to earth, to suffer and to die for our sakes. I assure her of my love for her, my great interest in her, my sympathy for her in her sufferings, and my desire to help her. She weeps so much that I feel obliged to discontinue my talk lest she injure herself. When, finally, she is calm again I ask her why she did not take my medicine, and why she refused the nourishment which I had prescribed. At this question she puts her little emaciated hands together in a respectful salaam and says, while her voice trembles with emotion: " O, doctor, Sahiba, do not ask me to take your medicine! Do not ask me to take the nourishment! If I take your English medicine,

5

and if I take the food which you have prescribed
for me, I shall get well; and, O, I do not wish to
get well! So don't—please don't—ask me to take
it!"

'Tis thus in heathen darkness
    Fair women crave to die;
Their crushed and broken spirits
    From direst fetters fly.

Such mute appeal, unheeded,
    Must rend the startled air
Till God, in mercy stooping,
    Avenge that silent prayer.

O, haste, ye Christian people,
    Of every clime and name,
Go bear the Gospel message,
    Its joyful news proclaim!

Haste, haste, the day is passing,
    The harvest ripe appears;
List to thy Master's calling,
    Dispel all selfish fears.

Go, lift the purdah curtain!
    Go, break the iron bar!
Beat down that wall of granite,
    And shout the tidings far.

BOOK II

IN THE ZENANA HOMES
OF INDIAN PRINCES

TO

THE BELOVED SON OF MY ADOPTION

MR. J. A. ILAHI BAKSH

OF

THE HIMALAYA MOUNTAINS

INDIA

THIS SMALL WORK

"IN THE ZENANA HOMES OF INDIAN PRINCES"

IS

AFFECTIONATELY DEDICATED

BY

HIS EVER FAITHFUL AND TRUE

MOTHER-FRIEND

THE AUTHOR

IN THE ZENANA HOMES OF INDIAN PRINCES

THE TAJ MAHAL

THE Taj Mahal, of world-wide celebrity, is situated in the Northwest Provinces of India, about two miles from the city of Agra, on the bank of the Jumna River, and one mile east of Agra fort. It is an extraordinarily beautiful mausoleum, and was built by the Emperor Shah Jahan as a sepulcher for himself and for his favorite wife, Muntaz-i-Mahal, the " Exalted of the Palace," who died in 1629.

The cost of this temple is said to have been about two crores of rupees (about ten million dollars) and twenty thousand workmen were incessantly employed upon it for a period of twenty-two years.

The general design of this tomb is extremely complex and graceful, and the workmanship is most elaborate and remarkably beautiful. The chief features of the building are the mausoleum in the center, on an elevated platform, surmounted by a magnificent dome, with smaller domes at each corner, and four very graceful and exquisite minarets one hundred and thirty-three feet in height. The building is, for the most part, constructed of pure white marble from Jeypore and red sandstone from Fatehpur Sikri. The mosaic work of the interior is remarkably rich and beautiful in effect. This is the finest building in India, and is acknowledged to be the most exquisitely beautiful structure in the world.

A colossal gateway admits you to the inclosure. In front of the tomb is a beautiful garden, containing a great variety of tropical trees, in the center of which is an avenue of tall dark cypresses separated by fountains. From the foundation of the tomb arises a double platform, the first being of red sandstone, twenty feet high and one thousand feet broad; the second of marble, fifteen feet high and three hundred feet square. The whole building is about one hundred and eighty-six feet square.

The following description is taken from *The Times of India*, and was written by William H. Russell:

"On mounting to the platform of tesselated marble on which the body of the building, surmounted by its dome and slender minarets, stands, the proportions of the whole are so full of grace and feeling that the mind rests quite contented with the general impression ere it gives a thought to the details of the building—the exquisite screens of marble in the windows, the fretted porches, the arched doorways, from which a shower of fleecy marble, mingled with a rain of gems, seems about to fall upon you; the solid walls melting and glowing with tendrils of bright flowers and wreaths of bloodstone, agate, jaspar, carnelian, amethyst, snatched as it were from the garden outside and pressed into the snowy blocks.   Enter by the doorway before you; the arched roof of the cupola rises above you, and the light falls dimly on the shrinelike tombs in the center—see glistening marble again—a winter palace, in whose glacial walls some gentle hand has buried the last flowers of autumn.   And hark!   As you whisper gently there rolls through the obscure vault overhead a murmur like that of the sea on a pebbly beach in summer—a low sweet song of praise and peace.   A white-bearded moulvie, who never raises his eyes from his book as we pass, suddenly reads out a verse from the Koran.   Hark again! How an invisible choir takes it up, till the reverberated echoes swell into the full volume of the sound of many voices; it is as though some congregation of the skies were chanting their earnest hymns above our heads.

" The tomb stands in the center.   A dome of snowy whiteness, upward of two hundred feet above the level of the platform, with a circumference at the base of more than the same number of feet, rises above the great pediment which constitutes the shrine.   It is covered by two gilt balls, which are surmounted by a gilt crescent.   At each angle of the building a small dome, the miniature of that in the center, is placed.   There is an entrance on each side of the shrine formed by a very beautifully proportioned arch, with pointed top nearly the

height of the whole building, and smaller arches at
the sides. All this marble is wonderfully inlaid
with precious stones, with texts from the Koran,
wreaths of flowers, and the richest arabesques. It
is in the lower part of the building, and in the body
of the terrace, as it were, below the dome, that
the tombs of the great shah, 'the King of the
World,' and of his consort are placed. The ceno-
taph of the latter is covered with profuse ornaments
and texts from the holy book of the Mohammedans.
Her lord lies beside her, beneath a less costly but
loftier monument, and the two tombs are inclosed
by a latticed wall of white marble, which is cut and
carved as though it were of the softest substance in
the world. A light burned in the tombs, and some
garlands of flowers were laid over the rich imita-
tions of themselves by which the surface was covered. The chamber of the tomb is octagonal, and
is nearly in utter darkness. The effect of the rays
of the lamps on the white marble railing and on
parts of the glistening walls of the tomb is powerful
—gloomy and yet bright. On emerging thence we
once more enter the Great Chamber, where are
placed the unoccupied sarcophagus of the shah and
of his wife directly over the real tombs in the chamber below, on which are bestowed the most elaborate efforts of the extraordinary skill which is dis-
played in the building. Flowers in many gems,
mosaics, wreaths, scrolls, texts, run riot over the
marble surface of the sarcophagus, walls, and vaulted
dome rising above us."

THE ZENANA HOME is a small, dark, mud-plastered, unfurnished room where the high-caste and wealthy married woman is kept in lifelong seclusion.   It is, practically, a prison-house, a penitentiary cell, the tomb of a living wife.   Even the favorite wife of the Emperor Shah Jahan himself must have known no better home than this during her lifetime; but after her death the above-described extravagantly expensive monument was erected to her memory.

THE   TOMB   OF   THE   DEAD ⎫
                AND   ⎬ WIFE
THE   TOMB   OF   THE   LIVING ⎭

THE DEAD WIFE'S TOMB is grand and fair,
All wrought from snow-white marble rare;
By hand inlaid with mother-of-pearl,
Outlining flower and beauteous curl.
Its walls and ceilings all are fraught
With work mosaic, strangely wrought;
And rich and beauteous in design,
More graceful than a clinging vine;
While rainbow colors all combine
To glorify this dead wife's shrine—
A monument of stately grace
Whose brightness rivals heaven's face.
Its domes of shining marble rise
In bold relief toward the skies.
Full twenty thousand craftsmen wrought,
To hew from stone this wondrous thought,
For two and twenty years, they say,
Incessantly they toiled away
From early dawn till eventide;
They hewed, and carved, and beautified;
Nor did the daily task decrease,
Nor ever did the labor cease,
Till full one score of years and more—
One score and two—were counted o'er:
When, lo! the temple stood complete,
With grace and beauty all replete—

And wondering nations still confess
And marvel at its loveliness.
Ten million dollars, it is said,
Were spent for this tomb of the dead.

The tomb of *living wife*, I ween,
Zenana home of princess, queen,
Is small, and dark, and bare, and mean,
As lowest hovel ever seen.
The native's horse and goat and cow
More precious are, by far, I trow,
Unto his " royal " (?) heart than she
May ever hope on earth to be ;
She but his wife, and one of four—
Or one of many, many score.
And so she lives in living tomb ;
It is her "fate," her bitter doom ;
Unloved, unwept, she lives to weep
And lifelong, changeless vigil keep.
She prays to die, she sighs alone,
But no one heeds her bitter moan ;
      " Only a woman " she.

THE ZENANA WOMAN AND HER PURDAH HOME

ZENANA, properly speaking, means woman; but in a broader, more common sense it has come to be applied more particularly to the high-caste wealthy woman of India. Or it may mean her home, if hers can be called a home—the prison-house where she is kept in seclusion, the sepulcher where she must remain entombed during all the days of her life. Indeed, the term may be applied to almost anything which pertains to a native, high-caste wealthy woman of India or to her secluded life.

Purdah really means curtain, but in common usage it has come to be applied to the zenana home, or house; to the long, close garment which conceals the face and form of the zenana woman; or, indeed, to anything which contributes to the seclusion of a high-caste Indian woman.

We often speak of a " purdah woman," or we may speak of a " zenana woman " as being " in purdah." Both words relate to the custom of keeping high-caste native women of wealthy parentage in seclusion, but the word zenana relates more particularly to the high-caste wealthy native woman herself, while purdah relates to the environments which are adjusted with a view to her seclusion.

The very poor and the low-caste women of India, who greatly outnumber the wealthy, are as free as the women of any country; and may go out and in at their pleasure, carry packages on their heads from the railway station to European homes with the common coolies, sweep the streets, visit the parks with the children whom they have in charge, carry on regular laundry work—going for and bringing back the clothes themselves; indeed, they are free to engage in any occupation which belongs to their caste.

The daughter or the wife of a high-caste wealthy native gentleman, however, has no such privilege. She may never wander free over God's green sod.

She may never watch the advancing glory of the
rising sun in the eastern horizon nor gaze upon the
gorgeous sunset in the west.   Her foot may never
leave its imprint in the soft, moist sand of the sea-
shore.   She may not roam the woodland, nor pluck
the opening blossom laden with dew in the early
springtime, nor inhale the fragrance that fills the
air, exuding from every growing thing.   She may
never wander by the flowing stream, nor climb the
mountain height, nor rest in the shade of a tree,
nor breathe at early dawn the fresh, cool, perfumed
air that fills with joy and life and vigor every living
thing.   She is a prisoner, condemned to lifelong
solitude and close confinement, though guilty of no
crime; though innocent and guileless as an infant.

There is no chair in her home, no table, no furniture of any kind, no carpet on the mud floors of
her dwelling, no picture upon the mud walls; the
mud ceiling of her prison-house is festooned with
smoke only.   In the courtyard surrounding her
prison-house there may be an old, half-dead tree,
with its leaves withered and its branches broken.
There may be one or two horses, cows, or goats,
and a caged parrot also.   There is no grass.   The
place is surrounded by high brick or stone walls
plastered over with mud.   True, if her eyes are
strong enough to bear the terrible glare, she may
gaze upon the sun at the noon hour as he passes
almost directly over her head.   In the morning and
in the evening she may look up above her head and
see God's blue sky, but it is not the deep blue that

delights and rests the eye in this more temperate clime; that beautiful deep blue color seems burned out in the awful heat, so that the sky assumes a pale gray aspect, like a bleached and faded garment. During the monsoon weather she may watch the clouds, dark and threatening, as they pass above the dingy walls of her prison-house. Bouquets of cut blossoms may be brought to her to relieve the dull monotony of her solitary life, but this is all, or nearly all, that she is permitted to enjoy of all the numberless beautiful things which God has given to rest the eye and delight the human soul.

She is not, however, altogether alone in her solitude. She is one of many wives. If she be the first, or one, even, of the four chief wives, she is fortunate indeed. She may be only one of the hundred, or four hundred, concubines in her husband's harem; in which latter case she is nothing more nor less than a slave—purchased at a price—who may be kicked or beaten at the caprice of her lord and master, and upon the slightest provocation.

Who would not choose the hard, half-starved, overworked but free life of the poorest sweeper woman rather than the imprisoned, monotonous existence of a high-caste zenana woman, though hers be royal blood?

The Zenana Woman

She is a princess, or a queen—
She may not see, nor yet be seen.
She may not laugh, and shout, and play
Through childhood's buoyant, festive day.

She may not other maidens know
In youth, nor may she skip or row.
She has no toys with which to play—
No games to while the hours away.
She seldom hears a story new;
Of stranger guests she has but few.
She cannot knit, nor sew, nor brew,
Nor any other task pursue.
She cannot write, nor read, you know ;
To school she is forbid to go.
She may not with the poet soar,
Nor study any ancient lore ;
Nor scan a paper, or a book,
Nor even on a picture look.
Within four dingy walls of clay
She is forever doomed to stay—
Though guilty of no crime, I trow,
Her guileless heart and olive brow
Must feel a thraldom and a woe
Which free-born souls need never know.
She ne'er may wander glad and free
As any child of God should be.
Her foot may never tread the mead
Where cowslips grow and wild deer feed.
She ne'er may roam the woodland through,
Nor pluck the gentle violet blue ;
Nor trace the outline of a flower
Beneath some sheltered woodland bower.
Her foot elastic may not know
Nor feel the yielding sod below.
She ne'er may list the wild bird's song,
Where myriad feathered minstrels throng.
She ne'er may hear the echo fall
Within God's blue-arched forest hall ;
Nor breathe the clover-scented air,
Nor watch the bees their sweets prepare.
Her foot may never wander free
By any stream, 'neath any tree.

She may not climb the mountain steep,
Nor watch the cataract's fearful leap ;
Nor rest in peaceful valley green,
Nor gaze upon a beauteous scene.
She may not scent the new-mown hay,
Nor watch the golden dawn of day ;
Nor see the sun in glory set,
Nor pluck the blossoms, dewy wet ;
Nor breathe the perfumed morning air,
Nor gather shells and pebbles rare ;
Nor feel the thrill of dawning light,
Nor sadness sweet of gathering night.
The holy calm of eventide
Is all unknown where *such* abide.
Her pulses may not thrill and glow
To see the world clad white with snow.
She ne'er may see great forests bow
'Neath pyramids of snow, I trow ;
Nor may she see the giant trees,
Left naked by the autumn breeze,
All clothed in diamonds—as it seems—
And shining in the sun's bright beams.
She may not sail the deep sea o'er,
Nor press the yielding, sandy shore.
She may not list the ocean's roar,
Nor watch the eagle proudly soar,
Nor hearken to the laughing brook,
Nor slumber in a shady nook ;
Nor feel, nor see, nor hear, nor know
The wondrous marvels here below—
All things with grace and beauty fraught,
Which God's almighty hand hath wrought.
Her bleeding heart and aching head
Must rest upon a prison bed ;
Within four walls her life be passed—
Her ashes in the Ganges cast.

MR. SYED MOHAMMED, Aid-de-camp to His Excellency the
Nawab Khurshed Jah.

HYDERABAD, *November*, 10, 1887.

MISS SALENI ARMSTRONG, M.D.

DEAR DOCTOR: I have much pleasure in introducing to you Mr.
Syed Mohammed, Aid-de-camp to His Excellency the Nawab
Khurshed Jah. Mr. Syed Mohammed desires an interview with
you respecting medical attendance to the Begam of His Excellency
the Nawab.

I am expecting that your skill, under God, will restore the Begam
to health.

Most sincerely,

S. P. JACOBS.

The above letter explains itself. Shortly after
its receipt Mr. Syed Mohammed, accompanied by
several native physicians, was ushered into my
presence. They came to engage me as family
physician to His Excellency the Nawab Khurshed
Jah, of Hyderabad, Deccan. Accordingly, on the
22d day of November, 1887, several visits and letters having been exchanged in the interval, an ar-
ticle of agreement was drawn up and written on
English government stamped paper, according to
law, and signed by both parties.

The Nawab agreed to pay my professional fee of
seventy-five rupees per day, in addition to all incidental and traveling expenses of myself and servants, from the time of leaving home until my return.

As this agreement may be somewhat curious and
interesting in this country, we will here insert a fac-
simile of the original document:

I the undersigned Mohomed Hyder Physician to this Excellency Nawab Ameer Kabeer Khurshed jah Bahadoor do give in writing to Miss Salimi Armstrong M. D. of Bombay to the effect as follows; that in behalf of this Excellency I bind and agree with you to pay that during the illness of the Begum sahib whenever occasion shall require I shall send for you by letter or by telegraph to Bombay and it shall be your duty to start forthwith and in consideration of your so doing I agree to bear and defray all your travelling expenses such as Railway charges messing charges, Banghee rent and conveyance charges and one third class passage by Rail for a servant and I also agree to pay you in addition a clear sum of Rs 75 seventy five for each day on which your presence in Hydrabad may be necessary. Dated this twenty second day of November one thousand eight hundred and Eighty seven—per every 24 hours during your journey by Railway to Hydrabad of back to Bombay—

Witness
Narayen Deni amettjah   M Mohomed Hyder
Syed Khud hossein

Fac-simile of Legal Agreement, Written on Government
Stamped Paper.

EMISSARIES FROM HIS HIGHNESS SAGHT SING, THE MAHARAJAH OF BHINAI DISTRICT

On the 18th day of May, 1888, while in my great Khetwady Castle home and hospital in Bombay, a kind note from Dr. James Arnott, of the Bombay Medical College, announced to me the arrival of emissaries from His Highness Saght Sing, the Maharajah of Bhinai District; and presently my good butler ushered the gentlemen into my consulting office, where I sat alone with my interpreter, Mrs. Moses. There were three of them, all small-sized native men, each attired in a dress peculiar to his individual rank and country. It was a great medico-legal consultation case to which these emissaries had come to call me. Physicians were expected from various parts of India, and they wished me to make the journey from Bombay to Ajmere in company with one Dr. William Dimmock in time to meet the other physicians who would gather there. This I agreed to do in consideration of the, to the Maharajah, moderate fee of one thousand rupees and all expenses. This stipulation was readily agreed to, and the sum of one thousand two hundred and thirty-one rupees was paid into my hand in advance, with the understanding that any expense exceeding this amount should be met by the Maharajah before my return from Ajmere. Accordingly, on the 21st instant, I received the following characteristic native letter from Lachmi Narain, one of the emissaries and the private secretary to His Highness the Maharajah, a copy of which I here insert:

(An exact copy of original letter.)

DUNCAN ROAD, 21st May, '88.

DR. MISS ARMSTRONG, M.D., ESQ.,
Pyn Hospital, *Khetwady.*

Sir:

I have the honour to solicit your goodself that please make arrangements for going to *Ajmere;* because I have received the telegram to-day from *Ajmere;* so I beg to enclose its copy here for your kind perusal.

Will you kindl oblige me by letting me know that when your goodself have time after 4 o'clock this evening that I also may come to your Hospital.

Please drop a line or two about your journey settlement and oblige. Excuse trouble.

I am, sir,
yours most obdy,

LACHMI NARAIN, *Private Secretary*
to H. H. the Maharaja
of Bhinai in *Ajmere.*

FROM BOMBAY TO AJMERE

IN India, as in almost any part of Europe, one may travel first class, second class, intermediate, or third class, according to the proportions of the individual purse. The first class affords every comfort and luxury which the most exacting could desire, and is proportionately expensive. The first-class coach may open at the end or at the side. In either case before the train starts the doors are locked, and the first-class passenger is a prisoner in an elegant apartment, with broad, long, cushioned seats and a folding table, which can be extended at lunch time and closed afterward. There is also a very comfortable toilet room, provided with every convenience. On either side are the ordinary railway coach windows, provided with close shutters, which are usually kept tightly fastened during the hot season. In addition to these there is a large round hole in the center of each side of the car. This hole is filled with a thick, solid revolving wheel made of *cuscus tatti*, a fragrant grass or root peculiar to India, the lower half of which dips down into a deep trough filled with water. The wheel has a crank by which it may be turned around and around, thus saturating the whole of the *cuscus*. The hot air from without, passing through this wet, dripping grass, is cooled, and the traveler in the first-class compartment is comparatively comfortable. In some cases the *cuscus tatti* is arranged differently, the water dripping from above.

The second-class carriage is similar to the first-class, except that the carriage is somewhat old and worn and less elegant. It has, however, all the comforts of the first, and is provided with every convenience, while the expense involved is only half that of the first-class. Very few people in India travel first class—a native prince, or rajah, or some of the high English government officials, perhaps. The majority of the wealthy, even, travel second class, while the masses—thousands and thousands of poor people—travel third class; which is little, if any, better than a cattle car in America. Here the natives, with their filth, their food, their bundles, well-nigh innumerable, their *huq-quas*, and their babies, are packed together like cattle in a stall. The intermediate compartment, however, is an improvement upon the third-class, though far from being comfortable. It is a small place, about four by eight feet in size, having two narrow, straight, bare benches running lengthwise of the compartment—which is crosswise of the car. A narrow door opens at each end of the compartment. On either side of these doors there is a very small, narrow window. The floor is, of course, bare, and the ceiling very low. Altogether the place is small, crowded, dusty, close, hot, and very uncomfortable.

The expense of an intermediate ticket is just double that of a third-class and half the price of a second-class ticket, and by some it is laughingly designated "the missionary first-class," because the missionaries usually travel on an intermediate ticket. When, however, a physician is called to the home of a wealthy native that physician must travel first class if he or she would collect a first-class fee. If you take a second-class railroad passage to the home of a wealthy patient, that wealthy patient will invariably conclude that you are a second-class doctor. If you travel intermediate or third class, you will be regarded as a third-class doctor, or less than that.

In Bengal native baboos who have attended the Calcutta Medical College for one term, and who have failed in their examination, abandon the idea of any further study of medicine, return to their homes, and hang out a sign upon which is written words to the following effect: "Dr. Baboo ———; failed first year; fee, four annas"—that is, eight cents per visit. If he is so fortunate as to have successfully passed his first examination, he continues another term; and if he fail in the second examination, he will return to his home and announce himself as follows: "Dr. Baboo ———; failed second year; fee, eight annas"—that is, sixteen cents per visit. If he be able to get through the second examination and pass on to the end of the third year, and then fail, he will establish himself in practice with great confidence, and his sign will read: "Dr. Baboo ———; failed third year; fee, one rupee"— about thirty-three cents per visit. Thus is a physician's professional fee graded according to his qualifications. If you charge a small fee to a rich native, he will consider that you are a second or a third-class doctor. The larger your fee, the more expensive your method of travel, the larger your retinue of servants, the more trouble you require at the hands of your patients, the better your qualifications are supposed to be. A first-class doctor, it is commonly supposed, will charge a first-class fee, will travel in a first-class railroad carriage, and will be in all respects first-class, requiring first-class service from all his attendants. Therefore, while doing an immense amount of gratuitous practice for the poor, and carrying on a free dispensary for the lowest-caste people in Bombay, yet I charged a handsome fee when attending the rich native, and traveled first class on my way to his home.

Ajmere is a very ancient city of Rajputana, which is the capital of the British district, about two hundred and twenty-eight miles by rail southwest of Agra. It is situated in a very beautiful and picturesque rocky valley, and is surrounded by a stone wall, which has three large gateways. It contains several mosques and temples of immense architecture. The Dargah, or tomb of Knaja, the Mussulman saint, is much venerated. Many of the streets of Ajmere are broad and contain fine residences.

In 1891 Ajmere had a population of 68,843, of whom about 26,683 were Hindus, and 18,702 Mohammedans.

The journey from Bombay to Ajmere, a distance by rail of about six hundred and fifty miles, was a very tedious and trying one during the month of May, which is one of the hot months in this part of India. Fortunately, however, we arrived after sunset and were taken to a well-kept English hotel, where everything was done for our comfort. Huge *punkas* swinging from the ceiling of every room were kept in constant motion. Deep verandas surrounded the entire house. Every outside door had an extra hot-weather door, composed of solid *cuscus tatti*, thickly woven.   Upon each of these doors a bucket of cold water was thrown at short intervals during the day.   In this way the atmosphere of the rooms was made endurably cool, although the heat outside was so great as to render it hazardous for one to leave the house after seven o'clock in the morning or before six in the evening; and even at seven o'clock P. M., taking a drive up and down the streets of Ajmere, the air strikes the cheek like the heated blast from a furnace, parching the lips and rendering the eyes, nostrils, and mouth dry.

A CURIOUS MEDICO-LEGAL CONSULTATION

THE day for the consultation arrived; and at the appointed hour we were ushered into the presence of His Highness Saght Sing, the Maharajah of Bhinai District.   He seemed in every way a very ordinary Hindu.   He was not acquainted with the English language, and so, of course, I conversed with him through my interpreter, whom I had taken with me from Bombay.   The medico-legal question related to a young son, about a year old.   The Maharajah claimed this child to be the son of his second legal wife; but the Maharajah's brother disputed the matter.   The Maharajah had been married to this particular one of his chief wives for many years, but she had nevere borne him any children; and the Maharajah's title, estate, and all honors and wealth therewith connected seemed

destined to go to his nephew, his brother's son.
At length a male child was born in the home of
this Maharajah, and he announced that Her Highness Sarupkanwar Bai, the Maharani of Bhagore,
his second legal wife, had borne him this son.
Doubts as to the truth of this assertion were entertained from the beginning by his brother and
others. At length the matter was brought to trial.
Several medico-legal consultations had been held
previous to this occasion, but in each particular
case the several doctors had disagreed in their
diagnoses, and their certificates had proven unsatisfactory. On the occasion of which we are writing
the lady physicians from the Punjab, Calcutta, and
other parts of India, who were expected, either disappointed the Maharajah altogether or arrived too
late for the consultation. Consequently I was
obliged to conduct the examination alone as, of
course, the gentlemen physicians were not allowed
to see the queen nor to enter the apartment which
was occupied by her.

Her Highness Sarupkanwar Bai, the Maharani, is
a very tall, large-framed, and heavy Hindu woman.
I found her in a rather large room, which was, however, entirely without furniture. It had a bare ce-
ment floor, with mud-plastered walls and ceiling.
The place was so dark as to make it difficult to conduct
a satisfactory examination. The queen was surrounded by a large company of native women—
friends, relatives, personal attendants, and servants.
She was dressed as she appears in the accompany-

Her Highness Sarupkanwar Bai, The Maharani of Bhagore
(A Hindu Queen)

ing portrait, and held in her arms the young heir whom she claimed to be her son. She related to me the sad and pitiful story of her life. She told me that she had been sterile, and that for this reason her husband had hated and abused her in the most cruel manner.

As I conducted the examination to the best of my ability under existing circumstances, Dr. Dimmock, who had accompanied me from Bombay, stood outside of the locked and bolted door and called to me from time to time, asking the medical questions relating to the case which it was necessary for us to record, I shouting back the answers as rapidly as I was able to ascertain the true condition, my interpreter also taking notes.

When the consultation was all over a lady physician from the Punjab arrived on the scene. She had delayed in order to obtain her fee in advance, about which there had been a great dispute.

After returning to our hotel I dictated to my interpreter the certificate, describing the condition of our patient as I had found it, and Dr. Dimmock signed the certificate with me. I never heard the result of the trial, and do not know whether or not the young son was proven to be the rightful heir to the Maharajah's title and estate.

On account of the late arrival of the lady physician from the Punjab Dr. Dimmock and myself were detained in Ajmere longer than was at first arranged for, being away from our homes in Bombay for a period of five days, instead of three, as was at first anticipated. In consideration of this undue detention in Ajmere His Highness the Maharajah paid me a further sum of eight hundred rupees, in addition to the one thousand two hundred and thirty-one rupees which I had received in advance. This sum of eight hundred rupees he sent to Bombay for me during my absence in Hyderabad, as will appear in the following letter from Lachmi Narain, his private secretary:

(An exact copy of original letter.)

BHINAI, 15th June, 1888.
Rajputana.

DR. MISS SALENI ARMSTRONG, M.D., ESQ., *Bombay.*

SIR: I have the honour to inform you that, I had been to *Bombay*, after your leaving *Ajmere*, in the beginning of this month; but I am very sorry that I had not pleasure of seeing you, as your goodself was at *Haïdrabad.*

I had given 800 eight hundreds to Dr. Dimmock & took the certificate.

I hope I shall have the pleasure of seeing you there in the meantime; if God will help me.

Please give my best regards to Miss L. L. Seity your asisstt & also to your interpreter.

I hope your goodself are in the best enjoyment of good health. I shall be more lucky to hear from you about your welfare. Please drop a line or two & oblige.

Rao Sahib with kind regards.

I have the honor to be Sir, Yours most obor

{ Kindl use }
{ for address }
          LACHMI NARAIN, Pt Secretary to H. H.
          of *Bhinai* Distt. Ajmere,
                    Rajputana.

P. S. Kindl also send the receipt othe sum of Rupies 1231 *which* was given by me to your goodself, for your fees of Ajmere Journey.

A PROFESSIONAL VISIT TO THE HAREM OF
A MOHAMMEDAN PRINCE

WITHIN an hour after my return to Bombay from Ajmere I received a telegram from His Excellency Nawab Khurshed Jah, of Hyderabad, Deccan, calling me to that city for the purpose of treating his favorite wife, the "Mad Begam," as she is familiarly called.

The Nawab is a Mohammedan prince of great influence, being second only to the Nizam himself in power, in position, in wealth, and in influence.

Hyderabad is a characteristic native Mohammedan city, and is the capital of the Nizam's dominion of the same name, a great native or feudatory state, which occupies the larger part of the Deccan, or central plateau of Southern India, situated between the provinces of Bombay and Madras; and a distance of about three hundred and ninety miles by rail northwest of the latter city.

Hyderabad is six miles in circumference, and is surrounded by a stone wall, flanked by bastions. In 1891 it had a population of 415,039. It is one of the principal strongholds of Mohammedanism in India, and has many mosques. Hyderabad stands on the right bank of the Musi, and is 1,700 feet above the sea. The population consists of diverse elements, though nearly all Mohammedans, and is full of warlike spirit, nearly every man, woman, and child being armed with swords, knives, and daggers of various Indian device. It is said

that upon very slight provocation these Mohammedans will thrust a dagger to the heart of a friend
or neighbor.   A foreigner found within the city
walls is liable to be murdered for the sake of a gold
or silver ornament upon his person or a few rupees
in his pocket.   Murder is a common occurrence in
Hyderabad, and the guilty are seldom brought to
justice.   On the day of our arrival, however, we
saw seventeen Hyderabad men with their feet in
chains and their hands fastened behind them.
They had been arrested by the English government, were guarded by English officers, and were
being taken into Bombay for trial under charge of
murder.

It is really hazardous for any foreigner—English,
European, American, Hindu, or non-Mohammedan
—to pass inside the walls of Hyderabad city except
under the immediate protection of armed soldiers
wearing the uniform of the Nizam or of some well-
known Hyderabad prince.   Indeed, many instances
are recorded in which foreigners have ventured
within the city walls unguarded and never been
seen again.

The railroad station is situated outside of Hyderabad city, as the railway is not allowed to enter
that native center.

Upon my arrival I was met at the railway station
by the Nawab's servants.   For my conveyance he
had sent three splendid English phaetons, the
principal one of which was drawn by four thoroughbred English horses.   The Nawab had evidently

expected that I would bring with me a large retinue of servants, many personal attendants, and a large amount of baggage.   Instead of which I had only my interpreter, and, as for baggage, only my small medicine and instrument bags; so that the one fine carriage, drawn by the four horses, was quite sufficient to accommodate us both with all our luggage; and the other two fine phaetons, with their four prancing steeds, followed on behind empty.   There were to each carriage two coachmen, dressed in fine uniform, two footmen, and many soldiers, attired in the very handsome and striking uniform peculiar to the Nawab's soldiers; so that we had soldiers running on ahead, following behind, and running along at either side of our carriage.

The poor natives who thronged the streets seemed to recognize the Nawab's soldiers and fine equipages, and the way was quickly cleared for us in advance.   After driving through many of the chief streets of the city we finally came to the great wall which surrounds the Nawab's estate.   The armed soldiers who stood guard at the great gateway in this wall were ready with low salaams to admit us to his excellency's spacious grounds, and presently we drew up in front of the broad steps leading up to the Nawab's European palace. These steps were like those of a court house or some large public building rather than the entrance to a private residence.   The house itself is a large two-story building, with great, deep verandas surrounding it on all sides.   Several servants, in their pure

7

white native garments and scarlet sashes, waited
on the front steps to receive us, and the chief of
these, the butler, ushered us into the spacious hall
of the second floor, and left us alone to make ourselves at home. Before leaving us, however, he
acquainted us with the fact that this building was
kept expressly for the entertainment of the Nawab's
English and European guests; and that the place
was ours while we remained in Hyderabad, supplied
with a retinue of servants awaiting our orders.

THE NAWAB'S EUROPEAN PALACE

IT is an immense place; the ceilings are very
lofty and the rooms exceedingly large. The entire
palace is European in style and furnishing—at least
as far as oriental ideas permit. Any European,
however, would recognize native taste in the selection of the English furniture—sofas, chairs, and
other furniture upholstered in the most brilliant
blue, green, purple, orange, or scarlet velvet of the
finest quality; the carpets, brussels or velvet, of
the most brilliant tints; mirrors extending from
the floor to the lofty ceiling, and many feet in
width, surrounded by massive gilt frames; chandeliers reaching down from the ceiling with almost
innumerable prismatic pendants dangling and shining in the light.

The butler glides noiselessly into the room and
announces *khana* (dinner) ready, bowing low in a
respectful salaam. The great dining room is equally

elaborate and gaudy in its furnishing.   The long dining table, however, is neatly and tastefully spread.   No food is upon it except the fruit, and it is very tastefully and elaborately adorned with flowers in pretty English vases.

As soon as we have taken our seats the soup is placed before us, and after this follows one course after another, each of which we taste—the fish, the roast and vegetables, curry and rice, etc., etc., until, finally, the pudding and the fruit; after which, in real English fashion, the coffee is brought.   Dinner over, my interpreter and I seat ourselves in the large front veranda, where we can enjoy the beautiful grounds which surround this European palace.

The palace is surrounded by many armed soldiers, who walk up and down around the house, night and day, to protect the place and us.   They are clad in the handsome uniform peculiar to the Nawab's soldiers.

HIS EXCELLENCY NAWAB KHURSHED JAH

As we sit upon the veranda we see coming across the lawn several native servants of the Nawab bearing trays in their hands, and as they approach nearer we observe that these trays are laden with fruit of many kinds, fine and luscious.   Leaving their sandals on the ground, they mount the great steps, and coming to where we sit, they present the fruit, bowing low in a respectful salaam.

Later on we see other servants coming, bearing trays laden with flowers, and the above-described

ceremony is gone through with by these also. Once
again we see servants coming from the Nawab.
This time they bring large portraits—one representing the Nawab in his royal dress, another representing the Nawab in his everyday costume counting his
Mohammedan prayer beads and surrounded by his
bodyguard of nine men, and in the third picture
we have the full-length portrait of the Nawab's only
son and heir, His Excellency the Nawab Shums-ud-
Dawlah Shums-ul-Moolk.

An hour or so later His Excellency the Nawab
approaches, followed closely by his bodyguard armed
with many knives, swords, and daggers of various
native device. The Nawab is a short, somewhat
corpulent, elderly gentleman, with gray hair, kind,
intelligent eyes and a face with very few lines, but
which you would judge to be the face of one pos-
sessed of much true refinement and strength of
character. He is dressed in pure white garments,
including a small *pugrah*. His feet are bare, but
as he crosses the lawn he wears sandals, which he
will drop from his feet before he steps upon the
veranda of his European palace.

After a very kind and somewhat flattering greet-
ing his excellency describes the many painful symptoms of his favorite wife's very serious and com-
plicated diseases, and declares that she is so dear to
him that he would gladly spend all his fortune for
the sake of seeing her fully restored to health. He
would willingly feed her upon diamonds, rubies, and
pearls if he were sure that such a diet would prove

His Excellency Nawab Khurshed Jah, of Hyderabad, Deccan
In His Royal Dress

beneficial. I assure him that these precious jewels,
though beautiful to look upon, and great in their
intrinsic value, are yet quite worthless as articles
of diet, and could afford his wife no nourishment.
After dwelling at some length upon the exact physical and mental condition, past history, and present
symptoms of his wife, he invites us to visit her in
her zenana palace. In order to do this we must
pass through several lawns, gardens, alleys between
high walls, courtyards, and gateways, the latter being guarded by armed soldiers.

At length we come to a small, low gate in a great
wall. This gate is guarded by women. As we
halt here the bodyguard of his excellency the
Nawab quietly retires, and we are left alone with
the Nawab and the women in front of the little gate.
The Nawab now fumbles among the folds of his
white garments, and presently produces a huge brass
key, with which he unlocks the immense brass padlock by means of which this small gate is made fast.
The gate swings open, and the Nawab invites me to
pass through. In order to do this I must step up
and bow down—almost crawling through this hole
in the wall, as it really is. My interpreter crawls
through after me, and the Nawab himself follows.
The Nawab now closes this little gate, and fastens
it on the inner side with the same great brass padlock and brass key which were used on the outside;
and thus we stand, prisoners, within one of the
zenana homes of this native prince.

Looking about we see that we are in a somewhat

large courtyard—possibly one hundred by one hundred and fifty feet in size. The walls surrounding us are very lofty, so that it would be impossible for any man to scale them. They are stone or brick, I do not know which, plastered over with mud.

At the end near where we entered there are several small rooms, which are evidently occupied by the women-servants who throng the place. The two long sides have opening into them many great doors, like old-fashioned barn doors, which are fastened at the top with huge padlocks—all of them being now closed and locked. Each of these doors, as I learned afterward, opens into a tiny dark room of about ten or twelve feet square, having no windows and no furniture of any kind. The floor, walls, and ceiling are plastered over with mud. Each particular one of these rooms belongs to some one or more of the Nawab's one hundred concubines, who reside within this enclosure.

The space between the walls—the open court—is very much littered. It has no grass on the dusty ground, which is rough and irregular. In the center there is the relic of what must have been at one time a fountain, but it has long since fallen into disuse, and is now only a wreck. In one corner may be seen the skeleton of an old tree. At the further end of this inclosure there is a deep veranda —so deep that it requires many pillars here and there underneath, at short intervals, to support the roof. The floor of the veranda is covered with a grass matting, woven by hand from reed grass.

The whole veranda seems thronging with women-
folk—old and young, handsome and plain, large
and small, strong and decrepit—one hundred and
one, all counted.   We cross the open courtyard and
approach the veranda.   The Nawab drops his
sandals from his feet, and steps upon the matted
floor of the veranda.   My interpreter, who wears
European dress, sits down and removes her shoes
and stockings from her feet, intimating to me that
I am expected to do the same.   I hesitate, and my
interpreter explains to the Nawab that I never go
with bare feet in any home, whereupon he courte-
ously requests me to allow my shoes and stockings
to remain upon my feet, which I am glad to do.

The Nawab now takes us to the center of the
veranda, where, sitting with crossed legs upon the
floor, we find the little " Mad Begam."   Begam is
a title and means princess, or the wife of a prince
or nawab.   The one hundred concubines stand
about in respectful silence; they never sit in the
presence of the Nawab.   The little princess on the
floor is introduced by the Nawab, and I take her
hand in American fashion.   The Nawab now seats
himself on the floor by her side, and invites my interpreter and myself to do the same; but, observing
a hesitancy on my part, the Nawab immediately
arises, orders a chair to be brought, and stands
until it comes; this through respect for me.   After
much hurrying to and fro, and much vain searching, the little gate having been opened and a
servant sent elsewhere in search of a chair, an old,

broken kitchen chair is finally brought from somewhere. It then apparently occurs to the Nawab
that it is not courteous for him to sit upon the floor
while I occupy a chair; and, therefore, he com-
mands that a second chair be brought. After
another delay of equal length and confusion another chair is finally produced, and we sit down
comfortably near the little Begam; the Nawab,
however, drawing his feet up and sitting with his
legs crossed in native style, as he would do upon
the floor.

HER EXCELLENCY THE BEGAM SAHIB

THE "Mad Begam," as she is familiarly called
by the Nawab's almost numberless servants, personal attendants, concubines and wives, is a short,
somewhat stout little woman of about forty. She is
not a pretty woman, but has, nevertheless, a very
attractive face and evidently a strong personality.
Her wealth of long black hair, fine as silk, hangs in
two straight braids down her back, nearly reaching
the floor as she sits. Her great brown eyes are full
of a strange, hopeless sadness and longing. Her
countenance rarely changes in its expression, which
is that of settled, hopeless melancholy. She is not
originally a high-caste woman, nor has she always
been a princess, nor always lived in a wealthy family, nor has she always been confined in a zenana
home. She is a woman of low caste by birth, and
of poor parentage. In her childhood she was a serv-

ant to one of the Nawab's chief legal wives, and he
fell in love with the little low-caste servant girl, who,
in those days, was allowed to run out and in freely
and without constraint. He then took her to be his
wife—to be, indeed, one of his four chief wives; for
every Mohammedan is allowed to have four, each of
whom is supposed to be a proper and legal wife. He
may have many concubines also. Of course, when
this little servant girl was exalted to the position of
a princess, the chief wife of a Mohammedan prince,
she was then doomed to close seclusion and confinement of the strictest kind in a zenana home. The
first wife, who was this little girl's mistress in the
beginning, became madly jealous, and soon thereafter died, it is said, of a broken heart.

I have a talk with my little patient, the "Mad
Begam," and she seems to grow more and more
interested in what I have to say, asking many questions. When I sing, however, she weeps much and
finally begs me to desist, declaring that she cannot
endure it; and this notwithstanding the fact that
she cannot understand a word of the song, which is
in my own English tongue.

ANOTHER STRANGE MEDICAL CON-
SULTATION

AFTER making a very careful and thorough examination of my little patient I explain to the Nawab
that his wife has no organic disease; that her heart,
lungs, liver, and all the organs of her body are quite

sound; that the distressing symptoms which he has observed are of purely nervous origin and are the result of her manner of living—seclusion, lack of exercise, monotony, want of fresh air and sunshine, etc. The Nawab declares that we must have a consultation at once; and he immediately sends a servant to call the six native physicians who are in his constant and exclusive employ. These men have been educated in England, are thoroughly qualified, and are his family physicians, receiving from him a handsome yearly salary. They come immediately, in answer to his summons, and wait outside of the little gate until he shall be ready to admit them.

Ninety-six of the one hundred concubines now flee away, each of them hiding herself in the particular little dark padlocked room which she claims as her own, or perhaps shares with another. The remaining four of the concubines bring four immense rugs, and each of the four takes hold of one corner of two rugs, standing around the little patient in such a manner, holding the rugs above their heads, as to conceal entirely from outside view not only the little patient who sits in the center between them on the floor, but also their own persons.

When these preliminary arrangements are satisfactorily adjusted the Nawab admits the six native family physicians through the little padlocked gate into the zenana courtyard; and they all cross over to the veranda, drop their sandals, and come and take their seats on the floor near my chair. I then kneel down on the floor, just outside of the hanging rugs,

put my hand under the lower margin, and covering the tiny hand of my little patient with my own
large palm, I draw her wee wrist to the edge and
place the finger of the doctors, each in turn, on the
pulse of my patient, until all have an opportunity to
count the pulsation for themselves, and this without seeing any part of the Begam's person.

The native of India takes it for granted that
physicians are so clever and so skillful in the practice of their profession that they are able to know
and understand the exact condition of the brain,
heart, lungs, spleen, liver, and every other organ of
the body by the simple heart-throb as felt at the
wrist.   Fortunately, however, for the doctors in this
consultation, I had been able to make a more thorough examination, and could tell them the real condition, as I had found it by a minute, careful, and
thorough search.   When I had given this full explanation we all agreed in our diagnosis and pro-
nounced the disease hysteria.   This was not so
difficult a matter as the selection of appropriate and
acceptable remedies proved to be.

I had brought with me from Bombay my little
medicine bag, containing a variety of useful drugs.
On this occasion, however, I found it quite useless.
His Excellency the Nawab Khurshed Jah would not,
under any consideration, use one particle of medicine from my bag.   It had been compounded by
Christian hands and contaminated by Christian
handling, and would therefore break the caste of his
wife and family.   He had a huge medicine chest of

his own, which was now wheeled out from one of
the dark rooms adjoining this veranda. We find
that this medicine chest contains almost every phar-
maceutical preparation and remedial agent named in
the British Pharmacopœia.

I suggest a simple, efficient remedy, which I think
will meet the case and allay the most distressing
nervous symptoms. The Nawab immediately declares that he knows the drug, he has tried it, and it is
of no avail.   I suggest another remedy, and another,
and another, with the same result. Indeed I soon find
that the Nawab is well acquainted with almost every
drug contained in his medicine chest, and that they
have all been tried and proven valueless, at least in
this particular case. I then suggest a combination
of drugs which, fortunately, has never been tried.
This the native physicians in consultation all in-
dorse, and the Nawab agrees to give it a trial. Of
course I must compound the medicine, as I have been
called all the way from Bombay to attend this particular case. The medicine is therefore prepared
by my hand, under the immediate eye of the Nawab
and his six doctors; each of whom watches me with
the keenest and most critical eye to make sure that
I do not, by any sleight of hand or otherwise, intro-
duce any drug of my own which I may have concealed about my person, or any water or liquid of
any kind which has been contaminated by the touch
of a Christian hand.

Formerly it was the custom in this home, and in
all wealthy high-caste native homes, to prepare

at the same time two doses, exactly alike, one of which was to be first taken by the doctor in attendance. Then, after a period of two hours or such a matter, if no ominous symptoms manifested themselves, the remaining dose was administered to the patient. Before my time, fortunately for me, this custom had been objected to by some attending physician, and, as a result, two of the concubines had been condemned to take the trial dose. Therefore on this occasion I was instructed to compound three powders instead of one. We had decided upon powders, because any liquid which has been touched by Christians or by any person of low caste can never be allowed to pass the lips of a high-caste native. Even a pill must have some liquid "sticking stuff" to hold it together, and therefore, under the circumstances, a powder was the only remedy that could be administered. Three powders I make, weighing and dividing and mixing each in precisely the same manner, and in the same proportions. This done, the six native doctors are allowed to withdraw; they pass out through the little gate, and we are again locked in. Now the rugs are dropped and two of the concubines come forward to receive one each of the powders. This they do without any apparent trepidation. I must now wait two hours at least to watch the result of these doses. At the expiration of this time, as no dire symptoms manifest themselves, with great fear and trepidation the Nawab permits me to administer the remaining powder to his favorite wife, the "Mad Begam." After this I must, of course, remain for several hours to watch the result.   During this season of waiting and watching the Nawab frequently interrogates his wife as to her feelings.   At length he becomes much agitated, begins to wring his hands, paces the floor in great agitation, weeps, counts his beads in prayer, falls on his face in an agony of anxiety and distress; and, finally, coming to me, he implores me to do something for the relief of his dear wife.   He is sure she must be suffering.   He can tell, by the sad cast of her countenance, that she is ill and in pain.

I am still somewhat of a stranger in India; and not being well acquainted with the ways and methods and characteristics of the natives, I believe this man to be entirely sincere and honest, and greatly alarmed, and so I assure him that there is no organic disease upon his wife; that she is not in any sense seriously ill; that the nervous trouble from which she suffers is due purely and solely to her secluded, inactive, monotonous life; that she may suffer in this way for many, many years, but that she can never die from this disease.   To my great astonishment His Excellency the Nawab does not appear to be relieved in the least degree.   He weeps the more, wringing his hands, pacing the floor, prostrating himself on the ground, and groaning aloud.   Finally he comes to me again and declares that we must have another consultation.   The ceremonies above described are gone through with again, and again, and again.   I remain in Hyderabad for two weeks.   During this time I meet the six native doctors in consultation several times each day, always in precisely the same manner and always with precisely the same result.

The little " Mad Begam Sahib " proved to be a very gentle, sweet, attractive little woman, possessing much real strength of character, and my sympathies were all with her. Who could blame her if, amid such surroundings, she had grown restive, fanciful, morose, irritable, jealous, ill-tempered even, and hysterical ? The wonder grew upon me that she did not under such circumstances go raving crazy mad, as you and I would surely do if imprisoned, idle, helpless, and in all respects in her situation. The fact is she was not " mad." Her reason had never forsaken her nor her mind lost its equilibrium in any degree. She was only nervous, irritable, jealous, and hysterical—unhappy, as all zenana women must be.

From morning until night, through all the days, weeks, months, and years of her life she is expected to sit quietly upon this veranda, without any occupation whatever. As intimated on foregoing pages, she cannot read nor write, sew, knit, weave, nor engage in any domestic occupation whatever. She is not permitted to bathe her own person nor dress her own hair nor make her own toilet. Has she not a hundred slave girls to do her bidding? They perform every service that she requires and wait upon her continually ; she may only take the curry and rice, which is her sole diet, in her fingers from the brass plate to her mouth. She has no toys to oc-

cupy her attention, no games with which to amuse
herself and those about her, no pictures to look
upon.

At one time, as the Nawab himself informed me,
he conceived the idea of erecting an art gallery for
the amusement of his wives and concubines. This
he did. The great picture hall was lighted from
above of necessity, as it must be a *zenana* place.
He sent to England for portraits of the royal family
and many other distinguished personages, and gathered from many sources portraits of eminent indi-
viduals, until he had a large collection, enough to
cover the walls of his art gallery. When all things
were ready he invited his wives to visit his new art
gallery. They did so; but as soon as they beheld
the faces of men and women hanging upon the
walls, having never before seen a picture, they took
fright and fled away in alarm, imagining that they
had seen ghosts and that these pictures must surely
be able to speak, to grasp, and to pursue. Never
again could the Nawab persuade any of his wives
to return to the " haunted hall."

THE NAWAB'S SIX PALACES

OSTENSIBLY and professedly I had been called from
Bombay to Hyderabad for the express and sole purpose of attending upon and treating this favorite
wife of His Excellency the Nawab. In truth, however, I did attend other members of the Nawab's
great family.

In the late evening, unattended by his bodyguard of nine men, without the knowledge of any of his personal attendants, without the knowledge of his favorite wife or of any of the one hundred concubines that serve her in the capacity of slaves, without the knowledge of any individual, save that of my interpreter and myself, I was conducted by the Nawab, quietly and stealthily, to visit his three other chief wives in his three other zenana palaces.

I found each of these zenana palaces precisely like the one I first visited, and which I have described, where his favorite wife resides. I found each one of these three chief wives surrounded by one hundred slave girls, who are the Nawab's concubines; so that His Excellency the Nawab Khurshed Jah has no less than four principal legal wives and four hundred lesser wives or concubines, each one of the four chief wives being attended upon and surrounded by one hundred of the lesser wives or concubines, who serve her as slaves in a zenana palace of her own like the one first described.

These other three wives, however, treated the Nawab with greater respect, apparently, than did his favorite wife, the " Mad Begam." None of the three ever sat down in his presence, though two of them were really ill and not properly able to sit up at all. To these three wives I was permitted to administer my own medicine from my own medicine bag and without consultation or ceremony of any

8

kind. I was, however, instructed to maintain absolute secrecy in regard to these visits, and to regard the whole matter as strictly confidential.

In addition to the four zenana palaces and the European palace already described, His Excellency Nawab Khurshed Jah has a private palace of his own, where he delights to entertain his English, European, and American guests. We had the pleasure of visiting this palace also. It is furnished in a more elaborate style and more gorgeously than the European palace; but it is not in itself so large as the former nor has it so many rooms.

In addition to the gorgeously upholstered furniture, chandeliers, huge mirrors, etc., the Nawab's private palace contains many curious articles which in themselves are interesting specimens of the lavish and unparalleled extravagance of a wealthy native of India. To illustrate, a clock in the Nawab's palace, reaching from the floor to the ceiling and studded with jewels, cost him, as the Nawab himself assured me, several lakhs of rupees. He also showed me music boxes brought from England which cost him fabulous sums of money.

Altogether we visited six palaces within the great walls which surround the Nawab's estate—our zenana palaces, the European palace, and the Nawab's private palace, where he entertains his foreign guests, the two latter being surrounded by beautiful lawns containing rare trees, plants, and fountains.

A DIET OF COSTLY GEMS

At the expiration of our two weeks' stay in Hyderabad the Nawab paid me the professional fee agreed upon and begged me to close my hospital in Bombay, settle my business there, and arrange to remain in Hyderabad as family physician to his household. He offered me a salary of one thousand rupees per month, together with the exclusive use of his European palace free of rental, and all its staff of servants to be paid by himself. I declined his offer, because I loved the work for the poor which I was doing in Bombay and because I love medicine. Everything in connection with the practice of my profession is a pure delight to me. I could not feel willing to spend my life in the manner in which I had spent the last two weeks. I was not willing to act a farce, nor to make the practice of my loved profession a mere play, and so I returned to my home, to my hospital, and to my charity practice in Bombay.

Later on, when the Nawab visited Bombay, I met several of the native doctors in his employ whom I had met in consultation during my visit to Hyderabad. One of them informed me that after my departure from Hyderabad the Nawab had called a native doctor from a distant city, to whom he made the same remark in regard to feeding his favorite Begam upon jewels which I had heard from him. This native doctor replied that he was delighted to hear the Nawab express himself thus, as pulverized

gems was just the remedy that would surely avail
to cure her disease.   He had feared to advise such
a course of diet an account of the enormous expense
which it would involve, but if his excellency were
really willing to expend so much money for the sake
of restoring his wife's health, her recovery would
be certain.   When the Nawab assured the physician
of his willingness to do this the doctor immediately
returned to the distant city and procured a machine
for grinding diamonds, rubies, and pearls.   Upon
his return to Hyderabad the jewels were dropped
into a little opening in the top of this machine; a
crank was then turned and grinding ensued.
Presently a shining powder was emitted from a
certain troughlike exit, and this shining powder
was divided into doses and administered to the
favorite Begam at specified intervals.

Doubtless the diamonds, rubies, and pearls
dropped straight into the pocket of the native
doctor, and, most probably, the Nawab suspected
the truth, for he was too much of a native himself
not to see through such a deception; but for the
sake of deceiving his wife, for the sake of making
her believe that he was wasting his fortune upon
her because she, and she only, was the one woman
who held his heart's best affection, therefore he
was willing to seem to be deceived himself and go
to the enormous expense necessarily involved.

During this same visit of the Nawab Khurshed
Jah to Bombay I received from him a box of Hyderabad weapons, together with a brief note, bear-

ing the Nawab's coat of arms and his own signature, in the Hindustani language.

(An exact copy of original letter.)

MAHALUSUMRI STATION, 21st February, 1888.

To DR. ARMSTRONG, M.D., *Khartwodi.*

DEAR MADAM: Once, while you were in Hyderabad, I remember, you expressed a desire for some of the Hyderabad weapons, so I have send for some of the arms from Hyderabad for you, which I send herewith per bearer. I hope you will like them.

Hoping you are in the enjoyment of good health,

Yours sincerely,

KHURSHED JAH.

_____

HIS EXCELLENCY DEWAN LUCHMAN DASS, EX-PRIME MINISTER OF KASHMIR

ON the sixth day of December, 1889, I received a telegram from His Excellency Dewan Luchman Dass, ex-Prime Minister of Kashmir, calling me to the native town of Eminabad to attend upon his two wives, Dalie and Molie Luchman Dass.

A run of two hours by rail from Lahore, Punjab, brings me to the small railroad station of Kamoki. Here two of the Dewan's English menservants— Mr. Gerard, the Dewan's private secretary, and Mr. Bowden, his horse trainer—meet me, and I am driven in a fine, large English carriage, drawn by two thoroughbred English horses, to Eminabad, where the Dewan resides in the great old zenana home built by his father in the prime of his life and during the years of his greatest prosperity.

Passing two or more small native villages, we at length approach a high stone wall surrounding the Dewan's gardens. Driving along on the outside of this wall, we at length enter a road passing down between two very lofty stone walls, and presently alight in front of a massive gateway opening through one of these walls. This gate is always securely locked and bolted on the inner side.

Here His Excellency the Dewan himself meets us, dressed in a handsome costume which is neither purely native nor purely English, but really is a native costume modified to suit English style.

The Dewan is a large man, nearly six feet in height and somewhat corpulent, but exceptionally fine looking and prepossessing in appearance, and his native European costume becomes him well. He is a high-caste Hindu, is well educated, both in his own and in the English language, and is very clever. Indeed, he is recognized as the most clever and efficient prime minister Kashmir has ever known. His father was immensely wealthy, but he left his property to his widow, the Dewan's mother, who still lives in the old home near her son. The Dewan is a great spendthrift, getting through several lakhs (hundred thousand) of rupees in a single year. Now, however, that he has spent the larger part of his own personal fortune, he is largely dependent upon his widowed mother for support, and she wisely and with a jealous hand metes out to him a certain monthly allowance.

The Dewan, on this occasion of my first visit, re-

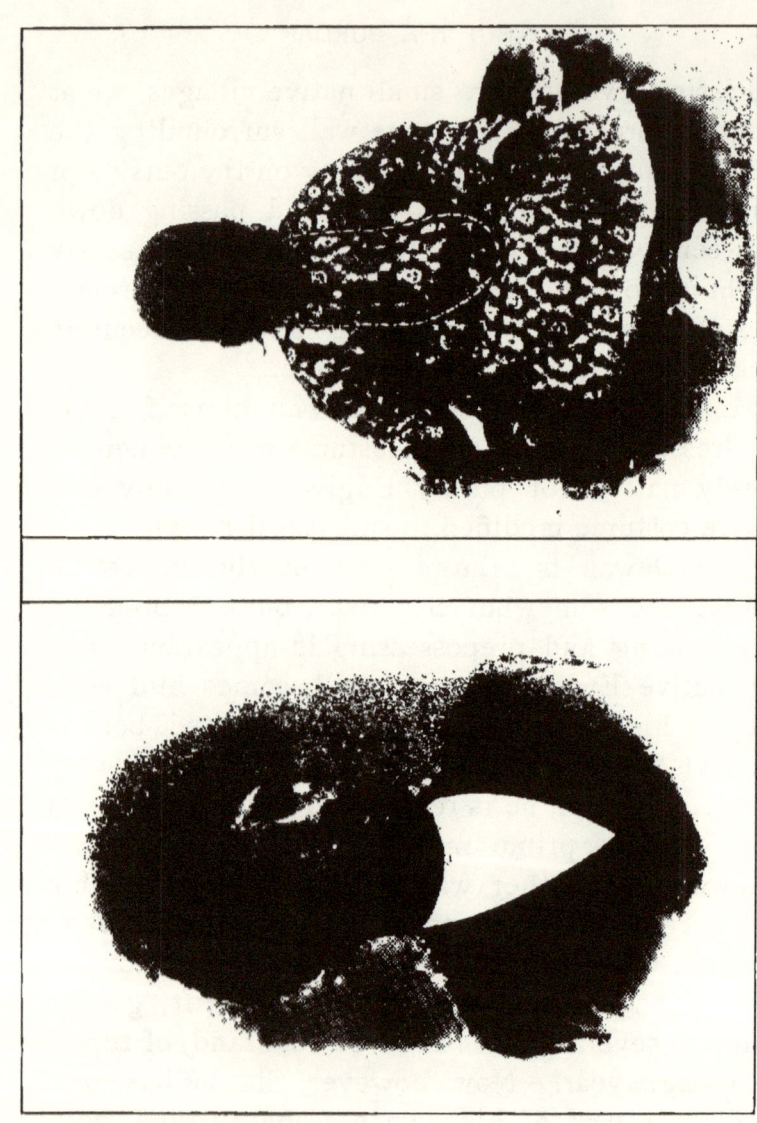

His Excellency Dewan Luchman Dass, ex-Prime Minister of Kashmir, and his Daughter

ceives me with that courteous hospitality, cordial
warmth, and respectful politeness which is a characteristic of the wealthy high-caste native gentleman.   This formality over, we alight from the carriage and crawl through a small square gate in the
lower part of the great gate, which remains locked
and bolted.   This tiny gate is again locked behind
us, and we find ourselves in a rather small and
much-littered courtyard.   Crossing to the opposite
side, we come upon an immense veranda leading by
several doors into a great hall capable of accommodating several hundred people.   Here we meet Mrs.
Gerard and other members of the Gerard family.
Presently the Dewan conducts my interpreter and
myself up several flights of stairs, each of which is
extremely narrow, steep, broken, and irregular.
Passing through several halls and narrow passages,
we finally emerge into a lighter place, and find ourselves in a very large, deep veranda, projecting
from the third or fourth story of this immense
building, and entirely surrounding the four sides
of the square courtyard which is in the center of the
building.   Walking around this veranda, we are
finally conducted through several small, rather dark
rooms, each of which is nearly empty, and at length
we are ushered into a rather pleasant apartment
about twelve by twenty feet in size.   Like all the
rooms we have seen in this great Hindu castle, the
walls and ceiling are entirely covered with gaudy
paintings representing hideous Hindu deities.
There are several chairs in this room, and a native

cot, upon which is a pure silk down comfortable and
a cashmeri shawl of immense size and fabulous cost.
Every four or five feet around there are small
square niches in the wall, forming shelves.   Upon
several of these shelves may be seen very exquisite
little English clocks, ornamented with costly gems;
and the whole apartment is littered with a large variety of rare and costly English articles—real sole-
leather trunks of the most expensive kind, real alli-
gator traveling bags, music boxes, and costly guns,
revolvers, etc.

THE WIVES AND DAUGHTER OF DEWAN LUCHMAN DASS

IN this Indo-European room we find the two native wives of the Dewan, Dalie and Molie, in their
beautiful and graceful pure silk Punjabi costumes,
and adorned with almost numberless pure Indian
gold (said to be the finest and most valuable gold
in the world) rings, bracelets, necklaces, anklets, toe
rings, and hair ornaments—all studded with costly
gems of many kinds, and almost priceless in value.

The Dewan's first wife died some years ago.
Dalie is his second wife.   She is a Mohammedan,
although the Dewan himself is a high-caste Hindu.
Of course he broke his caste in marrying a Mohammedan woman, but being a very wealthy man, with
influence, title, and position, this fact is ignored by
his people, and he continues to occupy a position at
the head of his caste.

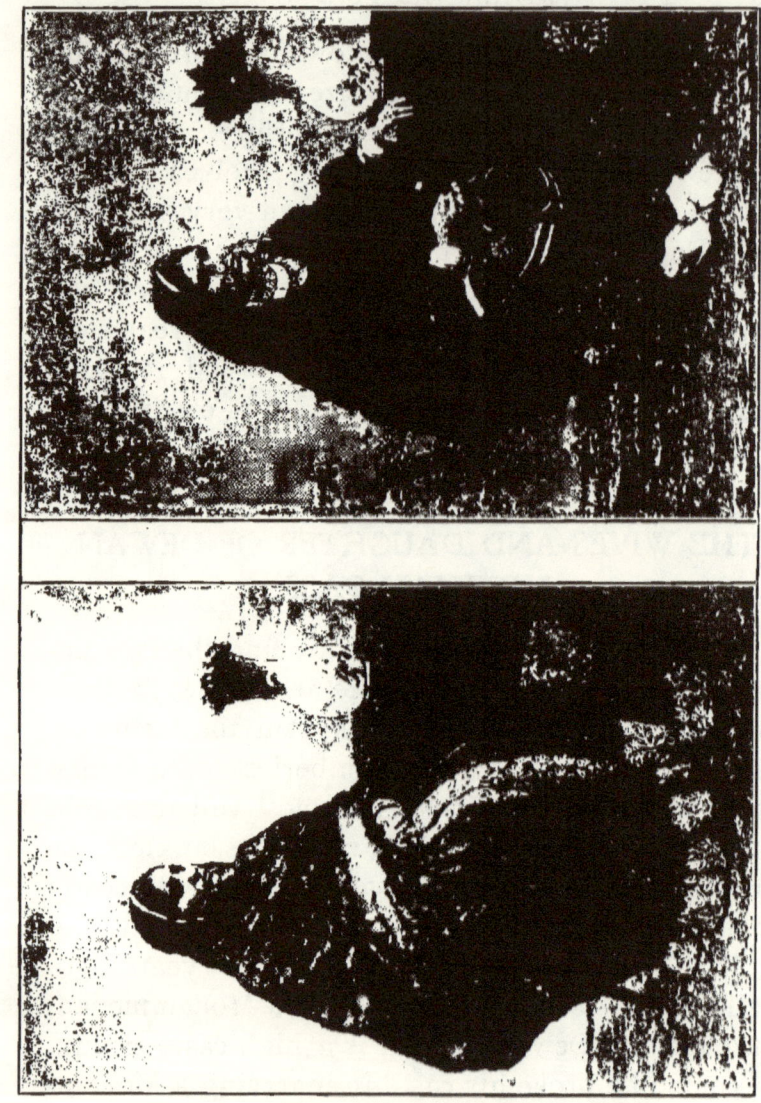

Mrs. Mollie Luchman Dass in her Kashmeri Costume   Mrs. Dalie Luchman Dass in her Punjabi Costume

Dalie, however, does not eat at the same table with her husband, nor touch his food, nor touch him while he is eating, nor touch any vessel from which he may ever take food. She sits apart by herself during meals, but near enough to her husband to be able to carry on conversation with him. She is the favorite wife, and her marriage was a love match.

Dalie is an attractive little woman, about five feet two inches in height, and weighing about one hundred and thirty pounds. She has a clear olive skin, large black eyes, long shining black hair, and beautiful hands. Her countenance is not, perhaps, beautiful, but is very attractive, intelligent, and kindly in its expression. She is conceded by all to be thoroughly unselfish, kind-hearted, and patient, and is universally beloved.

Molie is the Dewan's third wife. She is shorter and more slender than Dalie, with a fair complexion and a prettier face, but not equally amiable. The Dewan was married to Molie in accordance with the advice of the King of Kashmir and others in authority, because she is a woman of his own caste and of wealthy parentage, and in all respects deemed to be a suitable wife for His Excellency the Dewan.

Blanche Gerard is, in truth though not ostensibly, the Dewan's fourth wife. Of pure English blood, though born in India, Blanche Gerard Luchman Dass is the daughter of the Dewan's private secretary, and was bought for a price. She is a very pretty girl in both form and feature; graceful in every motion, and as beautiful in spirit and amiable in disposition as she is fair of face and graceful of motion. She loves the Dewan with all the intensity of her young, ardent nature, and is willing to sacrifice her life, good name, character, and even her soul for his sake.

Little Jannoo is the Dewan's only child. She is a beautiful, bright girl of six years, and the Dewan's idol. She is supposed to be the daughter of Dalie, whom she calls mamma, but she is, in fact, the daughter of the family laundress, who has served since Jannoo's birth as her nurse and servant. Little Jannoo addresses Molie as " Aunt," or, in the native tongue, " the sister of my mother;" while fair Blanche ostensibly holds the position of governess to Jannoo.

Such is the family of Dewan Luchman Dass. He has also many servants, more than one hundred in number. His possessions are very great. In addition to the immense castle where he resides, and which is more like a great town than a private residence, he owns in his own right some thirty villages, and all the land connected therewith and surrounding them for a distance of several miles. The rental from these villages amounts to more than one hundred thousand rupees per annum; and yet this sum is not nearly enough to satisfy the numerous wants of his excellency, and at frequent intervals he is obliged to draw large sums from his mother. The Dewan is considered to be a great spendthrift.   He owns many fine English carriages of various styles and fifty thoroughbred English horses, some of them being exceedingly valuable on account of their great speed.

MRS. LUCHMAN DASS, THE RICH HINDU WIDOW

MRS. LUCHMAN DASS, the Dewan's mother, was at this time supposed to be the richest woman in India, if not the richest individual.   She lives in one small room, like the one above described, except smaller, and without the signs of lavish expenditure for English luxuries which we observed in the former.   This little room is also on the third or fourth floor, but is in an entirely different part of the great castle.   Her dress consists of the one single coarse garment peculiar to the high-caste Hindu widow, only partly concealing her person.

Leading from this room, which is occupied by Mrs. Luchman Dass alone, there are several other small dark rooms, each of which is filled from the floor to the ceiling with pure gold and silver coin. The doors leading to these rooms are like great barn doors, and are all fastened at the top with great brass padlocks to which Mrs. Luchman Dass herself carries the keys.   Also underneath this great castle trenches have been made in which great iron tubes full of solid gold and silver coin are buried.   This was done by the Dewan's father.

The Dewan on one occasion took me over to pay his mother a professional visit. She was, at this time, a woman of sixty-five or seventy years of age, a bigoted high-caste Hindu. At the time of her husband's death she fain would have burned herself on his funeral pyre, but the English law prohibited all such acts of self-destruction. On this account, during all the years which have elapsed since her husband's death, Mrs. Luchman Dass has daily inflicted upon herself all manner of penance and privation, in token of her fidelity to her husband. She wears no ornaments of any kind, her hair is cut short, she takes but one scant and insufficient meal a day, and she inflicts upon herself many other tortures which I am unable here to describe. She allowed me to examine her carefully and thoroughly, but when I offered to administer certain medicines from my little medicine bag she immediately informed me that she could not, on any account, take any medicine from my hand, as she feared it might contain some liquid which would break her caste, coming thus from a Christian hand. I offered her medicine in the form of dry powder, but she still refused to take it. I then offered to bring drugs in dry form from Lahore, and compound the powder in her presence, but, although she consented to have me do this, she did it in such a manner as to make me doubt whether she really intended to take the medicine thus prepared.

After examining and prescribing for my poor rich patient I spent an hour or so in personal con-

versation with her—she talking freely about herself
and family.   Very soon she grew interested, and apparently gave me her fullest confidence, and as I
was about to take my departure she slipped upon
my finger a gold ring set with coral, which she asked
me to keep in memory of her.

I have now described my first professional visit
to the home of Dewan Luchman Dass and to the
home of his widowed mother.   On this occasion His
Excellency the Dewan engaged me by the year, for
an indefinite period of time, as his family physician,
and agreed to pay me the sum of six hundred and
fifty rupees per month in addition to all traveling
and other incidental expenses of myself and my interpreter.   Later on, however, the Dewan volun-
tarily provided me with a beautiful home in Lahore,
the second finest house in that town, all beautifully
furnished with rosewood and mahogany furniture,
Brussels carpets, rugs, china, pictures, and everything needed to render a fine house comfortable,
elegant, and homelike.   It also had spacious grounds
about it, with flower garden, vegetable garden,
servants' quarters, etc., etc., so that he estimated my
salary to be really equivalent to eight hundred and
fifty rupees per month.

In the course of the months while I was family
physician to Dewan Luchman Dass I became deeply
attached to Dalie, Molie, Blanche, and little Jannoo,
and much interested in the Dewan himself.   Indeed,
I had many long, earnest conversations with the
latter relating to religious matters, and he often

assured me that before he knew me he had lost faith in all religions, and neither believed in the Mohammedan, the Hindu, nor the Christian faith; but since his conversations with me and his acquaintance with my life he had come to believe in the Christian religion and to have faith in God and in the Lord Jesus Christ, assuring me that now he often prayed to God, in Jesus's name, asking for guidance, help, and blessing, such as I enjoyed myself and of which I had so often spoken.

The Dewan is an exceptional native in being a man of broad, liberal views.   He has adopted many English and European customs and habits of life. Unlike the ordinary wealthy native, he does not confine his women folk in strict zenana seclusion, and would gladly allow them to throw off the purdah altogether if they were willing to do so. Occasionally he takes his wives for a drive in one of his closed carriages, and it is said he sometimes takes them, in the late evening and by way of country roads, in an open carriage.   Of course in the latter case the ladies are concealed from public gaze by their close purdah garments, which fall from the head to the floor, entirely covering the person.

It was my custom to visit my patients at Eminabad two or three times a week, according to the need, but I was often called by wire for extra visits in cases of special emergency.   I found them always very kind-hearted, sympathetic, and affectionate. They fully reciprocated my affection and looked forward to my visits with great interest and pleasure.

Rare Trophies Described in Accompanying Pages.

1, 2, The Nawab's Sword and Dagger. 3, The Tiny Crimson Bag. 4, The Little Bag Studded with Mirrors. 5, 6, The Two Dolls Made by the Peer's Daughter. 7, The Gold Calendar Watch which belonged to His Highness Ahmed Singh, King of Kashmir. 8, An Indian Cot.

On the seventh day of October, 1890, the Dewan presented me with a valuable hunting-case, eighteen-carat gold watch, said to be worth about seven hundred and fifty rupees. The watch was originally a gift from His Highness Ahmed Singh, the King of Kashmir, to the Dewan, and bears the king's monogram on the front of its outer case. It is not only a watch, but is also a perpetual calendar, having in addition to the hour, minute, and second hands two little hands, one of which indicates the day of the week and the other the date of the month. The inscription, which is beautifully engraved on the outside of the inner case, reads as follows: "From Dewan Luchman Dass to Dr. Saleni Armstrong, Eminabad, Punjab, India, 7–10–'90."

October 13, 1890, I met with a railway accident which crippled me for a period of two and a half years, and obliged me to resign my position as family physician to His Excellency Dewan Luchman Dass.

Since the railway accident above referred to, and the resignation of my position as family physician to the Dewan's household, Mrs. Luchman Dass, the Dewan's mother, has died; her remains have been burned and her ashes cast into the waters of the Ganges. The Dewan being the only surviving son of his father, inherited his mother's immense fortune, and it is stated that he hauled fifty lakhs of rupees in solid gold and silver from Eminabad to the English banks of Lahore.

9

THE PEER

IT was a hot, sultry day in India, and, as usual,
I was very busy in the operating room of the Government Hospital of Hyderabad, Sindh, to which institution I filled the position of physician-in-charge
by English government appointment. Through the
open lattice work, which intervenes between the
great, broad pillars of the veranda and the reed-
grass chicks which curtain the open doors, I heard
an unusual commotion, and, looking out, saw the
servants, nurses, everybody about the place, rushing
from the back to the front of the house, where an
old, white-haired, long-bearded, distinguished-look-
ing native gentleman was alighting, with the supple-
ness and agility of a youth, from a fine Arabian
horse, blue-black and glossy as a raven's shining
breast.   He was surrounded by a bodyguard of
many Mohammedan men, all of whom were bowing before him as if in worship.   My Mohammedan
servants also, as soon as he had alighted from his
horse, bowed down before him until their foreheads
touched the earth.

Presently my interpreter, rushing into the hospital, exclaimed in a most excited manner, "The
peer is here and wants to see the doctor Sahib!"
" Give him a seat in my office," said I, "and let him
wait; I will be there presently." "O, doctor Sahib,
how can I ask him to wait? It is the peer, and he
seems in great haste!" "And who is this peer,"
said I, "who cannot be asked to wait?" O, he is

a very great man and a very great saint; all Mohammedans worship him and all Hindus seek his
life, and the English government is pledged to protect him; and he wears a sword and knives which
were presented to him by an English government
official; and he has authority to slay anyone who
dares to attack him." All this was rattled off in a
breath and in the most excited manner. "Well,"
said I, "you need not ask him to wait; I will go at
once."

As I entered my office I saw the peer standing in
the middle of the room in an attitude and with an
air which reminded me of a wild bird of prey which
had alighted upon the earth for a moment, with
half-poised pinions, ready to take flight at the
slightest alarm.

With the grace and courtesy of a knight of the
olden times he bowed himself when I entered,
kissed my hand, and told me that he was "a beggar;" that his daughter, the joy and delight of his
life, was very seriously, dangerously ill, and he had
come to beg me to go without delay to save her life.
He had no money to pay me, but he would give his
life, he would do anything for me, if I would only
save his daughter. When I consented to go the peer
spoke a word to one of the Mohammedan men, who
waited, bowing, at the door, and presently a dozen
Mohammedan men rushed off to engage a carriage
for my conveyance, and in an incredibly short time
many carriages drove up in front of the hospital
gate. It was not because I had ordered them, but

because the peer had need of a carriage, that so many came and waited and begged for the privilege of doing the service. Not for filthy lucre, not one of them would accept a *pie* (a small Indian coin worth about one sixth of a cent) from the peer for any service which they might be able to render. They consider him to be the greatest saint on earth; and esteem themselves most highly privileged if they are permitted to do him a service, and thus, perhaps, receive his blessing. The peer waited until he saw my interpreter and myself safely seated in one of the best of the carriages in waiting, and then he mounted his steed and fairly flew over the country, out from the city, over the country roads, and through the jungles to his home. It was well-nigh impossible for us to keep him in sight, although our coachman kneeled down in the front of his carriage and applied the whip to his already excited and running horses. Such a chase! Two or three times the peer was quite out of sight, and we feared lest we should not be able to find his home. Presently, however, we saw him standing, impatiently waiting for us to come in sight, then off again.

At last, in a most out-of-the-way place, such as one might seek for concealment, in the center of a jungle, surrounded by scraggy trees, we found him. He had alighted, and waited to assist me from the carriage. A great stone wall, so lofty that no mortal could scale it, surrounded his home. Opening through this wall there was only one gate, an immense, heavy, double-doored gate, which, however,

was always kept securely padlocked.   In the lower
part of one of the two doors which constituted this
gate a little traplike gate opened, through which
we crawled, after which this also was padlocked
behind us.

Within the inclosure are three very fine Arabian
horses; one of them black, a perfect match to the
midnight steed which bore the peer so swiftly from
our hospital, and two iron grays.   There are also a
goat, a tiny musk deer, several caged birds, and a
parrot.   At the further end of the inclosure is a
deep veranda, covered with matting and very much
littered.   This veranda admits us to the one tiny
room which constitutes the peer's home and that of
his two wives and his one daughter.

Before entering the peer gives me a seat on the
veranda, sits down beside me on the floor in native
style, and describes the condition of his daughter.
She is in a perilous condition of health.   Eats nothing, absolutely nothing, and frequently vomits large
quantities of fresh blood; he does not know how she
lives at all.   But he feels sure that my English medicine will be the means of restoring her health, in
which case he will worship me.   Her mother, who
was the peer's first wife, died several years ago.
This daughter is his only child and his sole earthly
solace.   She is the idol of his heart; he could not
live without her.   All this he tells me in the most
impressive manner, and begs me to spare no pains,
no trouble, no expense, but by all means to do something for the restoration of his daughter's health.

He is poor, so he says, a beggar upon the earth.
The fine Arabian horses were given to him as a
token of love by his followers. The costly gems and
exquisite ornaments which adorn the person of his
beloved daughter were all gifts from Mohammedan
worshipers. He has no money; he lives upon the
charity of his people; they send him food and provide for each and all of his needs as they occur.
Ask for it? No, never! He is a beggar in fact, but
not by practice. He would starve rather than ask
alms; it is not necessary for him to ask; his followers count it their chief joy and privilege to present
him with all material good. All this, by way of
explanation, comes from the peer's own lips.

My interpreter then explains that the peer is a
great prophet, and preaches his Mohammedan religion in the streets and everywhere wherever he
can get an audience, and that many people have
been converted from the Hindu religion to the Mohammedan through his instrumentality. On this
account the Hindus hate him and seek his life, and
have offered a great reward to anyone who will slay
him; but the Mohammedans worship him and the
English government protects his person.

The peer also explains to me that his daughter,
though sixteen or seventeen years of age, is still
unmarried. Not because there is no one willing to
marry her; on the contrary, any wealthy, high-caste
native Mohammedan man in India would count himself highly honored if permitted to marry the peer's
daughter. This is a very exceptional case; no other

like it in all India.   The peer has no equal in India, and there is no man in all that country worthy to marry the peer's daughter.   He has kept her un-married all these years, hoping that some great king or prince would come from a distance, asking for the hand of his daughter in marriage.   No such one having arrived, she is still unmarried.   " Is he, the peer, then, disgraced? " I inquire.   "O no! Nothing could disgrace the peer! "   " Is his daugh-ter, then, disgraced because she has passed the age of twelve and is still unmarried? "   " O no!   Noth-ing could disgrace her, because she is the peer's daughter! "   The gods could not curse her; she is not a Hindu, to be cursed by their gods, but a Mohammedan; and it is not her fault that she is still unmarried, nor her father's fault; but only be-cause there is no man in all India worthy of such a bride.   She is, therefore, allowed to wear her silken apparel, her gold and silver ornaments, with their costly settings, and her beautiful hair remains uncut, though she be unmarried and past the age of twelve.

THE PEER'S DAUGHTER

WE are now ushered into the one little dark room which constitutes the home of these strange people, and the peer introduces his daughter.   We find her reclining gracefully upon a low cot, covered with down quilts, soft silk spreads, and exquisite and costly Kashmeri shawls.   She is attired in the most delicately tinted pure silk garments, and is literally covered with gold and silver ornaments studded with costly gems. A more exquisitely beautiful maiden never lived in any clime or delighted any home. Perfect in form—neither tall nor short, neither thin in flesh nor stout, but just round and sweet and lovely. Graceful in every motion, prepossessing in appearance, and having in an unusually large degree that strange, rare, native dignity peculiar to high-caste Indian women. At first she seems languid. Her great, soft brown eyes are cast down and her transparent eyelids droop, while her long curling lashes almost entirely conceal from view that subtle light which flashes and gleams in their dark liquid depths beneath her father's searching gaze; for his eyes are like an eagle's in their keen, piercing stare.

I take my patient's tiny hand, so soft and delicate and exquisite in its contour, and find the pulse regular, strong, and perfectly normal in every way. The father looks away for a moment to speak to my interpreter. His daughter glances first at him and then darts at me a keen, intelligent, bright look, quite unlike the languid glance described above. With a few tender words the peer commends his daughter to my care and withdraws. As soon as he is quite away, and his daughter has heard the key turn in the padlock of the little gate, she immediately sits up and begins an animated conversation in the most intelligent, bright, and winning manner. No more is said about her illness. Of course I insist upon making a thorough examination, but

find heart, lungs, and every organ of her body in a
perfectly normal, sound condition.   The thermom-
eter marks no rise of temperature, and there is no
sign of disease upon her.

She puts innumerable questions; is interested in
everything I say; wants to know all about the
world outside, about America, about my home and
friends there, and how we live, and what it is like to
be free and to go and come at will, and innumerable
things.   Finally she begs me to take her home with
me, begs me to take her to the hospital, begs me
to take her anywhere.   She wants to see the world
and people and things.   The monotony of her life
is killing her.   She is a prisoner.   Her father loves
her, is devoted to her, idolizes her, but keeps her in
a living tomb.   He will not relent; he will not grant
her any liberty; he will not even allow her to peep
over the high wall that surrounds her home.   If
she could only climb to the roof of her house, as
poor, low-caste women are allowed to do, and have
a look, be it ever so little, round about outside of
her father's compound (lawn or yard), that would
be something.   Her father, however, is hard; he
will not allow her the least little peep of the outside world; she never sees anybody nor anything;
never is allowed any privileges nor liberty of any
kind.   She is "dying" to get away from this
wretched place.   She speaks pretty broken English,
and can read and write.   Her mother was an educated woman and taught her at home.   Her grand-
mother taught her mother in the beginning.   How

this small bit of education first crept into this native home is unknown, but certain it is that it has been appreciated, and has been extended from mother to daughter, so that this peer's daughter is able to read and has some idea of the outside world, although she has never seen it.   Nor has she many books to read.   Only occasionally some newspaper, or a scrap of some newspaper, comes within her grasp.   She assures me that she has read just enough about the world to make her crazy to see it.   How animated she seems!   How brilliant!   How her eyes flash and how the bright color deepens in her exquisitely rounded olive cheek as she speaks!   A fair and lovely picture to behold, here in her dark, dingy prison-house.   As she again and again begs me to take her away I feel obliged to suggest the diffi-culties, which she knows so well and feels so keenly. Then she falls back upon her low cot disappointed, sad, disconsolate.   Presently, however, she springs up like some wild thing and begins to tell me in the most impressive manner how very ill she is; how she has frequent attacks during which she vomits clear blood ; that she cannot eat ; that she goes whole days and days and days without a morsel of food; that she has no appetite at all.   For this cause I must take her to the hospital.   The change of diet, the change of surroundings, the nursing, and all will serve to restore her health.   I promise to use my best influence with the peer to induce him to send her to the hospital.   This I do, but he refuses; will not entertain the proposition for a

moment. Again and again, during the weeks that
follow, he comes on his black steed tearing over to
the hospital, and takes me back at the same break-
neck speed to visit his daughter, who has recently
had another attack of this terrible hemorrhage from
the stomach and has taken no food or nourishment
of any kind for a period of several days—a week,
perhaps. Finally, after many such trips, I succeed
in persuading the peer to bring his daughter to the
hospital. The time is appointed for the journey—
midnight, on the darkest night in the month.
First of all, of course, she is enveloped in her long
white purdah garment, which extends from the
crown of her head to the floor and trails about her
feet. Then she is placed in a closed purdah carriage—
a box arrangement, in which there is no window—
and the one door through which she enters is tightly
fastened. This box-shaped purdah carriage is then
raised by means of two long poles and carried on
the shoulders of four servant men. These men are
all high-caste Mohammedans, and the peer himself
walks along at the side of the carriage, keeping his
hand upon the door. Thus, in the middle of the
night, the peer's daughter is conveyed from her
zenana home to our zenana hospital. In the hospital she makes rapid improvement, eats well, and
vomits no blood; is happy as a lark, the very light
of the hospital and the delight of all its inmates; a
little wayward, however, regarding confinement.
She begs the nurses to allow her to peep out the
doors, walk on the veranda, and enjoy many other

little privileges of freedom. They, fearing the
peer, forbid all such innocent diversions. Then she
becomes imperious, and asks them how they dare
to refuse the peer's daughter! How they dare to
command her! Nevertheless, she submits.

Every time I visit my little patient in her ward
she entreats me to take her home with me. She says
she will cover herself completely from view with
her purdah garment, and then ride in my carriage
by my side from the hospital to my home. I dare
not grant her petition. Finally, one of the Mohammedan nurses, who worships the peer, thinking I
will surely yield and that I intend to take her over
to my house, sends a message to the peer to this
effect. The peer is furious, and, white with rage;
he tears over to the hospital, clinching the hilt of
his sword. Thus he rushes up to the hospital and,
meeting the matron at the veranda entrance, de-
mands to know where his daughter may be found.
She quietly assures him that his daughter is in her
ward, and that he can see her in a moment if he will
wait in the office. This unarms his rage in part,
but not wholly. He will stand and wait until his
daughter appear. When, however, he sees that
she is really there and coming he relents and tells
the matron, Mrs. Collins, and my native Christian
interpreter, Pareni, who has come in, that he came
with the full purpose of murdering them all, and
declares that he intended to kill the doctor Sahib
as well, in case he did not find his daughter at the
hospital. Finding her there safe and well, and

being assured that she shall not on any pretense be allowed to escape, he returns to his home satisfied. Some days later the peer expresses a desire to take his daughter home, believing her to be fully restored to health.   I acquiesce in this latter opinion, and agree that she may leave the hospital in the course of a day or two.   The news of this conversation soon reaches my little patient, and that evening she has a violent fit of vomiting and a terrible hemorrhage.   Of course the matron sends for me instantly.   When I arrive I find my little patient lying quietly in her bed apparently exhausted, but not more pallid than usual.   I take her pulse and find it perfectly normal.   The ward floor near the bed of the peer's daughter is badly stained with blood (?), the nurse having allowed the stains to remain until I should see it.   I request them to leave it until the following morning, when I shall be able to examine it by daylight.   In the morning I discover that the vomited matter is not blood, although I cannot tell what it is—something which has the color of blood, and which appears like it in every way, except that it does not coagulate.   I intimate to the nurse in attendance my suspicions, and order her to give my patient a bath without giving her any intimation of her purpose, and to make a thorough search for any red powder or liquid which may be concealed about her person. Soon after this the nurse who has charge of the peer's daughter comes to my home to report.   Her patient made all sorts of excuses in order to avoid

the bath, and made many other excuses to gain
time in order, as it proved, to get rid of something
about her person. In spite of all, however, the
nurse discovers a tiny bag fastened about her patient's waist underneath her clothing which contains
a red powder, and being hard pressed, the peer's
daughter confesses this red powder to be the substance which she swallowed in order to make it
seem that she had vomited blood. Of course she
confides this to the nurse in great confidence, exacting a promise of secrecy. She further explains
that her women servants bring her the powder
whenever she wants it, and that they also give her
food in her father's absence, thus enabling her to
fast in his presence.

Prior to this discovery the peer had been notified
of his daughter's illness, and he therefore decided
to allow her to remain in the hospital until such
time as she might be again fully restored.

Many such stratagems as these are resorted to by
the peer's daughter in order to obtain a greater degree of freedom, diversion, or change.

After many words, much entreaty, argument, advice, and every means that could be resorted to, the
peer is finally persuaded to bring his daughter to
my home to pay me a brief visit. Of course this
must be done after nightfall, on a dark night, and
in the same closed purdah carriage which conveyed
her from her zenana home to our zenana hospital. I
sit up until a late hour in order to receive my little
guest. It proves to be a very great treat to her.

She is delighted with everything she sees in my home. Of course all my male servants have been previously sent away from the premises, and there is no man about the place except my husband, who is cloistered in a room apart, and who receives the peer himself and entertains him during the visit. At a late hour the peer enters the room where we sit and announces that he is ready to return to his home and that his daughter must prepare to go. Almost instantly my little patient takes a severe pain, and invites her father to withdraw in order that she may make known to her physician the character of her sufferings.   As soon as the peer has left the room his daughter arises, shrugs her shoulders, smiles significantly, and continues her visit.   Still later in the evening she entreats me to keep her; to make some excuse to her father so that he will allow her to remain with me.   O, if she could only live here always!   Such is her cry.

Poor child! Just a healthy, strong, vigorous maiden, full of life, and health, and vigor, and energy, and interest, to whom all things in life seem beautiful, enticing, fascinating; and such a one condemned to lifelong solitude and seclusion!

After her return to her little dark zenana home our patient has frequent attacks of vomiting and hemorrhage like those above described, and on each occasion I am summoned to her side in great haste by her father.

The peer often visits us in our home; professes to be very fond of Mr. Hopkins and deeply grateful

to me for what I have done for his daughter. Sometimes he spends several hours at our home. On
such occasions, when his hour for prayer arrives (the
Mohammedans worship seven times a day), he goes
to the front of the house, spreads his garment upon
the ground, stands upon it, and goes through all the
ceremonies of Mohammedan worship. He usually
spends one hour at his prayers. This over, he goes
back into the house and engages in conversation
again with anyone of us who happens to be at
leisure. He usually brings some gift for me, from
himself or from his daughter. Thus, at one time,
he brought me the beautiful little musk deer, which
was his family pet. At another time he brought me
two lovely ringdoves.

When we were about to return to America the fact
somehow came to the knowledge of the peer's
daughter and she sent me an urgent request to visit
her once more before leaving India. I can never
forget that last visit. How sad she was at the
thought of never seeing me again! She presented
to me many little tokens of love. Among them
were two dolls, representing a wealthy high-caste
Mohammedan lady and gentleman of Hyderabad,
which she had made expressly for me, with her own
deft fingers; also a bag, studded with tiny round
mirrors and embroidered in silk floss of many colors.

The peer's daughter is, in two notable particulars, a very great exception to the ordinary high-
caste zenana woman of India. First, having passed
the age of twelve years unmarried, she is, neverthe-

less not considered to be disgraced herself nor a disgrace to her family and caste, and, secondly, she
has been taught to read and is able to do some sorts
of needlework with her own hands, and is allowed
to divert herself in this manner.

Strange as it may seem, the peer's daughter has
a lover, and one, too, whom her father does not
approve.

A short time before my first visit it happened that
a young native prince from some distant city came
to see the peer in regard to some matter pertaining
to their Mohammedan religion or worship.   While
he, the young prince, was being entertained by the
peer outside of the high wall which serves to keep
his wives and daughter in seclusion, one of the
servant women returning from Hyderabad city,
where she had been sent on an errand by one of the
peer's wives, saw this young prince and was much
impressed by his handsome face, courteous manner,
and grace and dignity of bearing.   When she was
again admitted through the small gate into the
presence of her mistress she was, as usual, interro-
gated by the peer's daughter as to all she had seen
and heard during her absence.   Of course she mentioned the fact of having seen this wonderful young
prince who was visiting the peer, and enlarged upon
his many charms, the fascination of his brilliant
eyes, the beauty of his raven locks, and the dignity
of his manly bearing.

The peer's daughter had never looked upon the
face of any man save that of her father only, as she
10

has no brothers and no near kinsmen. Upon hearing this description from the lips of her servant
woman she became frantic to meet this handsome
young prince, and began at once to devise means
whereby she might achieve this end. At length it
was arranged that there should be another errand
which would make it necessary for one of the servant women to go again to the city; and that, as the
peer unlocked the little gate to allow her to pass
out, one of his wives should call him urgently—the
daughter feigning sudden illness; meanwhile the
servant woman, rushing through the little gate,
should speak to the young prince, and give him a
hint of the true situation, asking him to return the
following day at a certain hour when it was known
the peer would be away from home attending to his
religious duties.

This arrangement was successfully carried out, and
at the appointed hour the young prince appeared
again on the spot and waited and watched for further developments. By some device of these fair
plotters, for the peer's wives and servant women
were in league with his daughter, a sort of ladder
was improvised, by means of which she, the peer's
daughter, climbed to the roof of her father's house
and from there looked over the wall which surrounded her father's premises, down upon the young
prince who waited to see her face. They were not
near enough to hold any conversation, but it seems
it was a case of " love at first sight," and mutual.
The young prince was completely charmed and cap-

tivated by the bewildering beauty of the peer's daughter, and the peer's daughter, on her part, fell madly in love with the prince.

Of course the peer must never know that his daughter's face had been seen by a man, and without divulging this fact the prince applied for the hand of the peer's daughter in marriage, but without success. The peer did not consider that this young man was of sufficiently high caste, sufficiently wealthy, or that he held a sufficiently exalted position in the world to be worthy of his daughter; and his decision was of course final. The young couple, however, continue to send messages, through the servants, each to the other, always hoping for a time to come when, somehow, all barriers to their union may be dissolved.

The little gate is never allowed to remain unlocked, not even for the space of a single moment, and no servant woman can leave the premises except she be passed out by the hand of the peer himself. This she may do occasionally, when there is some errand which can only be done by a servant woman or which is beneath the dignity of the peer. If she return during the peer's absence from home, she cannot be admitted until his return; she must wait without until the peer come and bring the only key which will unfasten the padlock of that little gate.

The young prince lingers about the place and watches, from some distant hiding place, for the peer to leave home, then draws nearer, hoping that some means may be arranged whereby he shall

have the opportunity of gazing once more upon the
face of the fair young maiden who has won his
heart. She, on her part, watches and waits for his
approach, longs for her father's disappearance, and
seizes every possible opportunity to behold the handsome face of her lover.

Should there ever be a sequel to this strange ro-
mance, which is not a fiction, but a fact, I may, perhaps, on some future day be able to "continue"
this story to its happy (?) termination.

Is there no release? Is there no release? O
God, is there no release? When shall these prison
walls be broken down? When shall these innocent
captives be set at liberty? When shall these chains
of adamant be severed! When shall these fair
limbs be unbound? When shall these beautiful
and innocent slaves be emancipated? When shall
these sepulchers be unlocked and broken through?
When shall these living wives and daughters be
released from these tombs of living women? Who
will answer?

"The Spirit of the Lord God is upon me; because the Lord hath anointed me to preach good
tidings unto the meek; he hath sent me to bind up
the brokenhearted, to proclaim liberty to the captives, and the opening of the prison to them that
are bound;

"To proclaim the acceptable year of the Lord,
and the day of vengeance of our God; to comfort
all that mourn;

"To appoint unto them that mourn in Zion, to

give unto them beauty for ashes, the oil of joy for mourning, the garment of praise for the spirit of heaviness; that they might be called Trees of righteousness, The planting of the Lord, that he might be glorified " (Isa. 61. 1–3).

A PROPHECY AND A PRAYER

THE rich the poorest are, I ween,
    And most to be deplored
Their hapless lot, behind the screen
    Where naught may joy afford.

The chains that bind are adamant;
    The walls are great and high;
The purdah veil remains unrent—
    Fair captives weep and sigh.

Our God shall break the captive's chain
    And set the prisoner free;
He'll rend the purdah veil in twain,
    That blinded eyes may see.
        Amen!   So let it be!

BOOK III
HEROES AND HEROINES OF ZION

" *Go ye therefore, and teach all nations, baptizing them in the name of the Father, and of the Son, and of the Holy Ghost:*

" *Teaching them to observe all things whatsoever I have commanded you: and, lo, I am with you alway, even unto the end of the world.*"—MATTHEW xxviii, 19, 20.

TO THE PEERLESS TRIO
MISSES HEWLETT, BARTLETT, AND CROSS
OF
THE CHURCH MISSIONARY SOCIETY
OF
UMRITSAR, PUNJAB, INDIA
WHO EXTENDED MANY KINDLY, HOSPITABLE
AND GRACIOUS COURTESIES UNTO
"ONE OF THE LEAST" OF HIS
EVEN AS UNTO HIM
THIS LITTLE WORK
"HEROES AND HEROINES OF ZION"
IS
VERY GRATEFULLY AND AFFECTIONATELY
DEDICATED
BY
THE AUTHOR

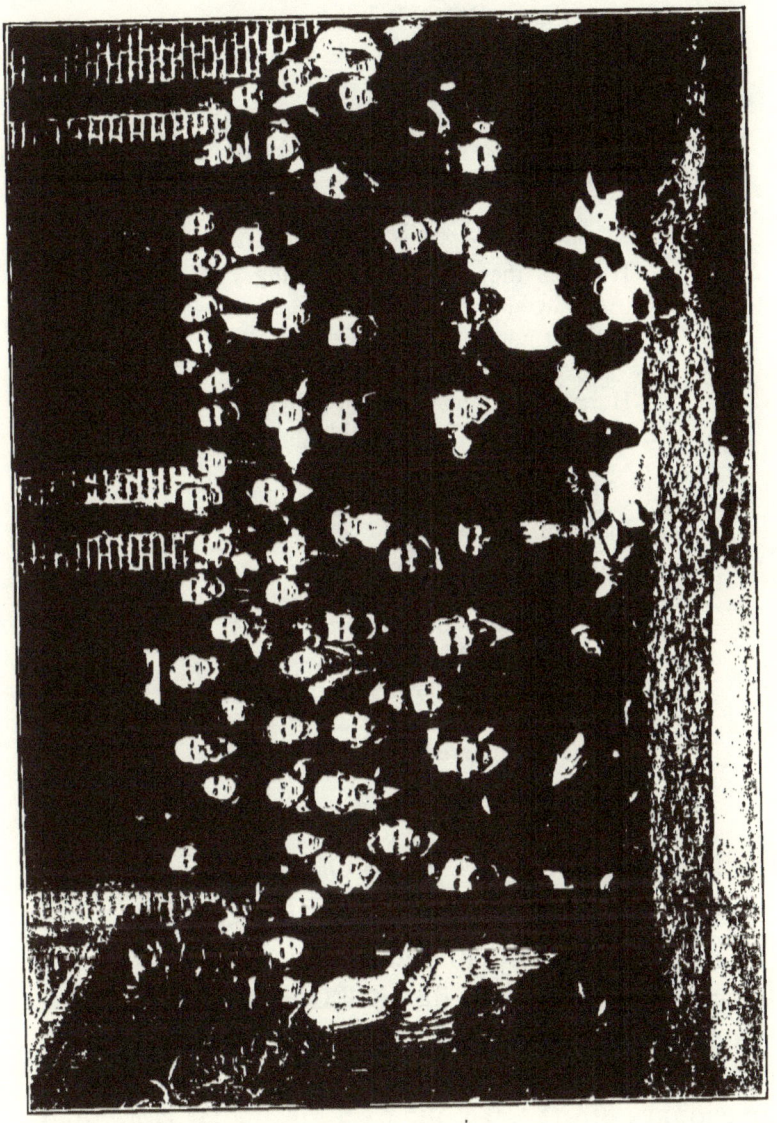

South India Conference

BOOK III

HEROES AND HEROINES OF ZION

WHO ARE THEY?

HEROES they who, self forgetting,
  Gladly yield their lives to God;
Seeking not for vain preferment,
  Meekly bowing 'neath the rod.
Heroes they, and heroes worthy,
  Who, neglectful of earth's gain,
Carry to the heathen nations
  Tidings of the Lamb once slain:
Slain for all mankind in common,
  Slain the nations to reclaim
From the dire results of sinning;
  Giving glory to his name;
Heroines and heroes noble;
  Worthy of our love sincere,
For unto the heart of Jesus
  They are cherished friends most dear.

THE METHODIST MISSIONARY OF THE PARENT BOARD

THERE are many phases of missionary work in India. Seventy-three distinct Christian denominations and societies are represented, and each one has many different branches and departments of missionary effort. In our own Methodist Episcopal

179

Church we have first of all the regular male missionary, sent out by the parent board and supported by our Missionary Society. Upon his arrival in India the first necessity which arises is that of mastering some one of the many languages spoken by the people of Hindustan. It will require one year at least for him to become sufficiently advanced in this study to be able to take charge of a native church. Usually, therefore, he is first appointed pastor of some English-speaking church. He may remain in this church for one, two, three, or more years; but whether it be a long or a short term of service, he is supposed to put in every spare moment in the study of the particular language which he has selected, and when he becomes sufficiently proficient to be able to hold conversation and to preach fairly well in the vernacular he is appointed pastor of some native church. Now his labors begin in earnest. Not only must he perform all the regular pastoral duties which devolve upon every pastor in the Methodist Church at home, such as regular Sabbath services, pastoral visitations, marriages, baptisms, funerals, etc., etc., but he must do much more than this. He preaches two or three times every Sunday, and usually once or twice every day in the week. At four, five, or six o'clock in the morning the butler (*hamal*) raps at the door of the missionary's bed chamber and cries out, "*Chota haziri, Sahib!*" (Little breakfast, sir!) At this summons the missionary goes to the door and receives a little tray containing two cups of tea or coffee, one for himself and one for his wife, and two or three thin slices of toasted bread already spread with buffalo butter—white as lard. There may also be two small bananas or two eggs, but these do not usually form a part of the little breakfast. Immediately after this "frugal meal," early, early in the morning, before the heat becomes too great for him to be out of doors with impunity, he is found on some public corner or square in the native bazar preaching the Gospel of Jesus Christ. This he may do even before he has become fluent in the use of the native tongue, through an interpreter. He takes with him one of his native local preachers or exhorters and they walk to the bazar together. As they approach the market place, or immediately after they arrive and have taken their stand, they begin singing some Christian hymn in the native tongue, and perhaps playing an accompaniment with cymbals, tambourine, or some other musical instrument of native device. This attracts attention and soon avails to draw a crowd. When a sufficient number have gathered the singing and playing ceases and our missionary begins his sermon. It is not a short discourse of twenty, thirty, or forty minutes' duration, but may last for several hours. The congregation is constantly changing; a few going away and others coming almost continually, so that at the close of the discourse, two or three hours after its commencement, the preacher will have an entirely different audience from the one with which he began. The service may be

varied from time to time, at the discretion of the
missionary, with song, prayer, scripture reading,
short addresses, or testimonies by native assistants.
Sometimes, especially in large cities, two or three
missionaries may go together to the morning street
preaching, taking with them several native helpers,
and in this case there will be several discourses, interspersed with prayer and singing. When the sun's
rays become intolerably hot the service is closed and
all return home, where they arrive usually at nine or
ten o'clock. *Bara haziri khana* (big breakfast) is now
in waiting—oatmeal, curry and rice, poached eggs
on toast, potato chips, bananas, and possibly beef-
steak. Breakfast over, the missionary conducts
family prayers. This he does sometimes in the
native language only, at other times using both the
English and native tongues, reading a part of the
Scripture lesson in our own language and a part in
the vernacular, or reading the same lesson in both
languages; praying first in one language and then
in another, or praying in the English tongue and
having his prayer interpreted sentence by sentence
into the native language. This is done for the
sake of the native servants, who have gathered
in the large dining room and sit around on the
floor with their legs crossed and their heads bowed
in the most respectful manner. During prayer
they will all lean over until their foreheads touch
the floor and remain in this bowed position until
the end of the Lord's Prayer, which all Christians
in the room repeat in concert. After family wor-

Butler Preparing Tea   The Ayah

Dena's Wife, the Ayah   Dena, the Butler
Miss Robinson   Miss W. L. Armstrong   Miss Levermore

Three Zenana Missionaries with Servants and Two of Miss Levermore's
Little Adopted Native Children, and Chung, Dena's Son

ship the missionary retires to his study, not for rest, but for letter or report writing, private devotions, or study.   At one o'clock the butler rings the bell, announcing that *tiffin* (luncheon) is ready.   This is a light meal, often cold—some cold sliced meat, a cup of hot tea, stale bread with buffalo butter, bananas, oranges, custard, apples, guavas, mangoes, or whatever fruit may be in season.   He may also have hot curry and rice, but this is not customary. After luncheon the missionary must see his local preachers, exhorters, and other native assistants, and instruct them as to the best methods of teaching the Scripture lesson, etc., etc.   At four or half-past four, the native assistants depart, leaving our missionary alone in his study.   Presently the butler, with bare feet, pure white turban of immense size, spotless *kurta* and *pacjama*, and scarlet sash, comes to the missionary's study bearing a small tray with a cup of India tea and a few English biscuits.   The missionary partakes of these refreshments with relish.   At this hour of the day, when the oppressive heat has served to enervate and depress the weary missionary, his afternoon tea seems a necessity.   In some missionary homes, however, the afternoon tea is dispensed with and dinner is served at that hour, in which case tea and biscuits are usually served late in the evening. At half-past four or five o'clock in the afternoon, as the heat begins to abate, the missionary leaves his home again.   This time he goes to the native city to visit his boys' schools.   Of these he may have a large number under his own care. A small upper room in the native city serves as a schoolroom, and a native Christian man, who has been educated in one of our missionary boys' boarding schools, is engaged as teacher. Native boys whose parents are heathen are gathered from all parts of the city to these day schools. Here the rudiments of an education are acquired and the pupils are prepared to enter English government schools of higher grade, but the Bible is the chief text-book and is taught regularly and carefully every day. There may be only one, but if there be ten, fifteen, or more such schools as this in the native city where our missionary is pastor of the native church, he must superintend them all. He visits each of them frequently, conducts all the examinations, directs and examines the native teachers, and has oversight and management of the whole. So that our missionary to India must be not only an able preacher of the Gospel and a consecrated Christian man, but he must also be strong and vigorous in body in order to endure the enervating effects of that most trying tropical climate and the strain of his incessant and arduous toil. He must also be a scholar, able to teach and to superintend many schools—to manage men, to marshal his converts; a very general.

Nor are these all the labors that devolve upon our missionary in India. He may have, in addition to the native day schools in the native city, one or more boys' boarding schools which he must super-

Rev. S. P. Jacobs with the Boys of One of His Native Schools

intend.   If his church be strong spiritually, finan-
cially, numerically, and in every respect, he will
have efficient helpers—class leaders, Sabbath school
superintendent, Epworth League president, stew-
ards, trustees, Ladies' Aid, and all the auxiliary
helpers which a pastor in a Christian land is supposed to have.   This, however, is exceptional.   As
a rule our missionary who holds the position of
pastor of a native church in India has little, if any,
efficient help in his church.   He or his wife must
superintend the Sabbath school, act as president of
the Epworth League, lead the classes, and fill every
position of responsibility in the church.

After our missionary returns from the native city,
where he has been to inspect or examine his boys'
day schools, he is usually ready for his *khana* (dinner), which is served at six, seven, or eight o'clock
in the evening, according to the prevailing custom
of the English people of the community in which he
lives.

No food is found upon the dining table when the
missionary and his family first take their accustomed places, except, perhaps, the soup, which
forms the inevitable first course.   After this, following in due course, come the fish, the roast and
vegetables, the curry and rice, and, finally, the pudding or the fruit.

Immediately after dinner the missionary conducts
family worship, the servants attending as in the
morning.

During the evening our missionary may have a
11

sermon to preach, an Epworth League service to conduct, a prayer or class meeting to lead, a Bible reading to give, a Missionary Conference to attend, some ill people to visit, or a report to write. In any case his time is sure to be fully occupied. And thus his busy days go by.

Besides the regular pastorates of the English-speaking and native churches there are other positions of trust and responsibility which must be filled by the regular male missionary of the parent board of the Methodist Episcopal Church. There must be presiding elders for the various districts, our Church papers must have editors and agents, our Christian schools and colleges must have presidents and teachers, our various printing and publishing agencies must be superintended by competent men, and at any Annual Conference session the regular pastor may be removed from his pastorate to fill any of the above posts left vacant by death or removal. Latterly, however, some of these important places, such as presiding elderships and professorships in our Christian schools and colleges, have been and are being ably and efficiently filled by native men. Indeed, some of our best Christian schools in India have but one or two American missionaries in their whole staff of teachers, and there are now many presiding elders in our native Christian Church who have proven themselves able, efficient, and satisfactory in every respect.

THE SERVANT QUESTION

SINCE my return to America strange reports have come to my hearing. A Methodist missionary is supposed by many to be a man of leisure who goes to India on a fat salary and lives at his ease, surrounded by servants to wait upon him. No greater mistake than this could be made. The Methodist missionary in India is an overwrought, overburdened, careworn man. That he bears his burdens and responsibilities gladly and cheerfully, as unto the Lord, does not alter the fact nor relieve the pressure which is surely telling upon the constitution and shortening the life. That he has servants to wait upon him is true. May I digress a moment while I explain this servant question?

Servants in India are a necessity. Not because the missionary is unwilling to work, not on account of laziness or idleness on the part of the missionary or his wife, but for reasons which grow out of and are dependent upon the caste system of India and other conditions which are peculiar to that country. To illustrate: You must have water to drink and for cooking purposes. Your cook will not bring it—he will not leave his kitchen for any purpose; the butler will not bring it—that is not his work; not one of the house servants will do it—they each have their own peculiar labor and will do but one thing; it is their occupation, their religion, their social standing among the people of their country, and—well—it is their caste! The *bihishti*

(water carrier) will bring water in a dressed goat-
skin on his back from some distant well, filling all
the water chatties in your house once, twice, or
three times per day, as may be needful. But suppose
you refuse to be thus served. You declare that you
cannot submit to having so many servants about
you, and you undertake to bring your own water.
Take a bucket, in the early morning, and start for
a distant well. You must start early, as in this
climate you cannot be out during the middle of the
day with impunity. When you arrive at the well (an
old-fashioned dug well, with a broad brick wall all
around which stands up four feet above the surface
of the ground), before you have time to climb to
the top of the brick wall, upon which you must
stand in order to drop your bucket down into the
well, several native *bihishtis* intervene and, with
low salaams and respectful entreaty, beg you to
desist. In spite of this you clamber to the top of
the brick wall and lower your bucket into the well.
The natives look upon all white-faced Sahibs (gentlemen) as their superiors, if not their lords, and for
this reason they do not resist you further, but stand
back in dismay while you pollute their well. After
your departure, however, these same *bihishtis*
gather about and fill up the well with soil and
stones. This is done lest by any accident some
high-caste native, not knowing that the well has
been polluted by the hand of a Christian, should
drink water from this same well and thus break his
caste. It may be that there is no other well for

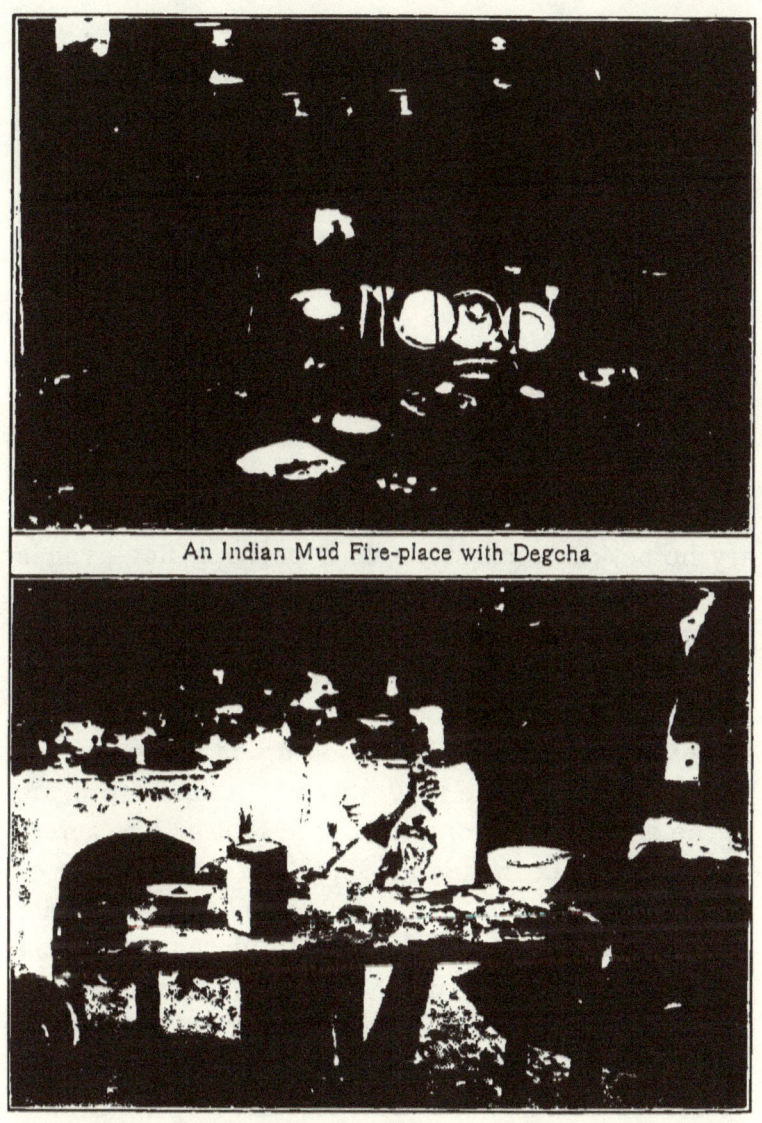

An Indian Mud Fire-place with Degcha

Domingo, the Cook, in the Kitchen of an American Missionary

some miles around, and this may create quite a panic for water, nevertheless the thing must be done—the well is ruined for native use, and forever. The next day you try again, and, finding this well filled up, you go to another. The same result will follow, until you are compelled to engage a *bihishti* to bring your water for you, which you can do for the nominal sum of from two to four rupees (sixty cents to one dollar and thirty cents) a month, and without board.

Do you suggest that the missionary's wife herself prepare the family meals, and thus save the expense of hiring a cook? There is no kitchen in the missionary home, no cook stove, and perhaps not even a fireplace, chimney, or stovepipe hole. The kitchen is some distance from the house, in the back yard. It is a small, dark room, with one door and one small square hole, with wooden bars crossing it, which serves as a window. The cooking is done on several little handmade mud stoves. These are made in the shape of a horseshoe, one foot or less across the top and six inches in depth. In the middle of the horseshoe the wood or charcoal fire is made, and on its rim, above the fire, is placed the *degcha* (a copper cooking utensil about the shape of an ordinary tin basin, only deeper, and of graduated sizes), which contains whatever food is to be cooked. Of course there is no pipe to this stove, and the smoke goes in the face of the cook and fills the room. During the hot season no English or American woman could cook in such a place as this without imperiling her life.

In some parts of India the above-described hand-made cook stove has been supplanted by an elevated fireplace or grate, built up with mortar and brick to about the height of an American cook stove and having several round openings in the upper surface which reach down to the open fireplace beneath. These are a decided improvement on the first-described stove, but having no chimney, stovepipe, or other means of escape for the smoke, they are still very unsatisfactory.

Thus it is with every department of domestic work. There are no modern improvements, no machinery, no conveniences of any sort. All domestic labor is performed in the same crude and laborious manner which prevailed in Bible times. For our missionary's wife to undertake to do her own housework in India would not only shorten her days, but would consume every moment of her time, every particle of her strength, and would thus render her incapable of assisting her husband in his missionary labors or of carrying on an independent mission work of her own, while for the nominal sum which one would pay an ordinary hired girl in America (say $2.50, $3, or $4 per week) one may support six, eight, or ten domestic servants in India and board none of them.

Besides this, for you to do your own work in that country offends the natives. They regard you as a low-caste, mean individual, who has come to their country to rob them of their rightful occupation and means of support. Moreover, having the serv-

ants in your own home affords another opportunity
of usefulness—you are enabled to show, to at least
your own servants, what a Christian home is like,
and to live before them a Christian life. They
gather at your family altar every day, hear the
Bible read and explained, and listen to the prayer
for them as well as for others. This is the most
powerful of all preaching, and it is a common thing
to see servants of the missionaries converted to God
and living upright Christian lives through the influence of their missionary master and mistress. Much
more could be said in regard to this servant question; indeed, a volume could be written in justifica-
tion of the practice of employing servants in India,
but more is unnecessary, except perhaps to intimate
the fact that the servants are paid from the private
salary of the missionary, and this expense therefore
brings no additional outlay to the Missionary Society
in the home land. The salary of a Methodist missionary in India is about equivalent to the average
salary of a Methodist pastor in America.

Many of our English-speaking churches in India
are entirely self-supporting, paying the entire missionary salary, all the incidental expenses of their
church, giving to the missionary cause, and in many
cases supporting native preachers and other workers
in addition; other English-speaking churches are
able to meet only a part of their own pastor's salary,
the remainder being paid by our Missionary Society.

Many of our native Christian churches, also, are
self-supporting, while others are so in part.

THE ASSISTANT MISSIONARY

IN America there are certain duties which devolve upon the wife of a Methodist pastor. She is supposed to fill a place in the church and community which is peculiarly her own, and in some cases, especially where she has a family of small children, and ill health, she finds the requirements by no means light, and at times the people of her husband's church seem to be somewhat exacting. In India, however, the wife of the Methodist missionary is herself also a missionary and has her own peculiar missionary labors to perform, although for these services she receives no separate, independent salary from any source. True, a married missionary receives a somewhat larger salary than the single missionary, and at the birth of each child the salary is again increased some fifteen or twenty rupees, and this sum may be supposed to meet all the actual requirements of his living expenses. It may be that the missionary's wife was formerly a regular missionary, sent out by the Woman's Foreign Missionary Society of the Methodist Episcopal Church and supported by them. Her salary was then equal to the salary of any unmarried male missionary supported by the parent board. On her wedding day, however, she ceases to receive her regular salary from the Woman's Foreign Missionary Society, and on that day she becomes an " assistant missionary " of the parent board. Her duties are designated by the Conference, and she is expected to report her work

in the regular manner. Her missionary labors require all her strength and all her time, so that, as
the little children come to her home, she is obliged
to hire an *ayah* (native nurse) to care for them.
Nevertheless, she receives no compensation for her
missionary labor except in the consciousness of helping on the great cause which she has learned to love
so dearly.

Is her husband's salary sufficient to meet all the
family needs ? Yes; under ordinary circumstances
it is. While both parties keep well and strong, and
there are no children to be educated, the missionary's salary is sufficient. If the health of husband
or wife become seriously impaired, the parent board
will pay their passage home to America, and possibly, in the former case, the husband may receive
half his regular salary during his leave of absence.
If, however, there are children to be educated, there
are no means sufficient to meet this emergency.
There comes a time when both missionary and missionary assistant break down in health and must return to their native land. In this case he must of
necessity take one of the small appointments in his
home Conference. He has been long away from
home, and there is now no place for him in his own
Conference. Younger men, who have been in the
Conference during all the years of his absence, have
crowded him out. He is now broken in health.
During his absence he has not been cultivating his
oratorical powers, but rather striving to simplify the
Gospel of Jesus Christ in such a manner as that the

ignorant natives could understand the message. He is not a "star preacher;" and the probabilities are that before he has been long in his native land he will be ranked among the superannuated of his Conference. In this case he has nothing laid up, and no income sufficient to support himself and family. Had his wife also received a salary for the work which she actually did for the parent board, as an assistant missionary in India, all this would probably be different. The injustice of such an arrangement must be apparent to all. And yet I never heard that any missionary's wife ever intimated a desire to receive compensation for her missionary toil, or dreamed that there could be any injustice in her being expected to give her strength, time, and labor to help on the great cause to which she and her husband have both consecrated their lives. On the contrary, she feels it to be a great privilege and joy to be permitted to thus spend and be spent for the blessed Master. Indeed, I very much doubt whether these noble, consecrated, self-sacrificing women would, at first, and readily, accept a salary from the parent board, even if it were offered. And yet is it not the least that we at home can do, to recognize the injustice, the self-sacrifice, and the heroism involved? Instead of circulating, or helping to circulate, a damaging report to the effect that missionaries go out to India on a fat salary, to live at their ease and to be waited upon by servants, should we not appreciate the fact that, while our Missionary Society pays a moderate, reasonable, sufficient salary for the service of one missionary, that Society actually receives in return for this one salary the consecrated, earnest, devoted service of two efficient missionaries instead of one. In the secular world no such thing would be expected or endured. If the husband is employed by any firm in this or any other country, he is paid for his labor, of course, and is paid a sufficient sum to enable him to support his family, but nothing is expected of his wife. If he fill a chair in any college or university, he only is expected to teach. If his wife take a class, or classes, she is paid for the labor which she actually performs. Why should not the missionary's wife be treated with equal courtesy and consideration, not to say justice? Perhaps you'll affirm, in reply, that the wives of missionaries are not all efficient workers; that many of them are not even thoroughly consecrated, earnest Christian women; that their work is by no means universally satisfactory either in quality or quantity; and that even the most efficient are liable to be disqualified for service by impaired health, household cares, and other domestic causes. All this we readily concede; but is it not equally true that when a young man presents himself to the Missionary Society of our Church as a candidate for the foreign field his wife's character and qualifications are taken into consideration almost as much as his own? And at each Annual Conference, when the appointments are to be made, is it not a fact that the qualifications and efficiency of the missionary's wife have much to do with the final

decision?   Certainly no reasonable person could require that a salary be paid indiscriminately to the
wife of every missionary who is employed by the
parent board of our Church.   It is only where actual service is rendered, and service which is acceptable and satisfactory to the board, that we feel
compensation is due.   Of course the Missionary Society must always be free to employ whom they will,
and to be judge of qualifications and of efficiency.

The missionary's wife, or "assistant missionary,"
as she is called by the parent board, has charge of
all the Bible women in connection with her husband's church.   They meet in her home several
times a week, and receive instruction from her.
This is practically a normal school on a small scale.
She teaches these Bible readers how to do their work,
how to read and expound the Scriptures to the native women whom they visit in their zenana homes.
Often she goes with them to these zenana homes,
teaches for them, sings and prays with the native
women, and has the whole under her immediate care
and supervision.   Besides this, she is also a zenana
missionary, and personally visits a large number of
zenana homes regularly, doing the same work that
is done by the regular zenana missionary who is supported by the Woman's Foreign Missionary Society,
except that she does not have assistant zenana
workers under her charge.   In many cases she also
has charge of native girls' schools, like the native
boys' schools which her husband superintends; and
she engages native Christian women to teach, such

as have been educated in girls' missionary boarding schools. She may have from one to a dozen or more of these day schools in the native city, for the daughters of heathen parents. She conducts all the examinations, keeps in touch with the teachers, visits the schools often, and superintends the whole work. In addition to this she may have in her own home a girls' boarding school, where she acts as matron, chief teacher, superintendent, friend, mother, and guardian to all the inmates. It is not usual that the wives of missionaries do street preaching in the public bazar; but some of them do this also, and with great success.

THE MISSIONARY EVANGELIST

THE work of the missionary evangelist, or pioneer missionary, in India is different from evangelistic work in America, although in some cases it may appear to be similar. The missionary evangelist, however, whose work we are about to describe, is not an assistant; he does not go to churches which are already organized and in good working order to hold revival services, and thus render assistance to the regular pastor in charge. He is an independent missionary, and a pioneer. He may be a presiding elder or the regular pastor of some native church, devoting himself to this specific pioneer evangelistic work during certain seasons of the year only.

In a canvas-covered cart or wagon, containing a supply of provisions for his own use, a small medicine chest, a few tools, a change of apparel, a supply of tracts for distribution—translated into various Hindustani languages—his Bible and hymnal, and accompanied by one or two missionary associates and perhaps several native Christian assistants, together with a servant or two, he travels from village to village, stopping at each place a few days or a week, as the work opens up before him or as each particular case may require, preaching the Gospel, distributing tracts, organizing churches and Sabbath schools, establishing missions, and healing the sick. There may or may not be a medical missionary in the company; in any case the missionary evangelist has sufficient knowledge of ordinary diseases and their remedies to be able to use to advantage a small supply of simple drugs, and the poor, suffering natives are glad enough to enjoy the benefits which they can derive from these medicines. There are no English physicians or surgeons in any of these native villages, nor are there educated native doctors; so that all the sick of the community are obliged to suffer on without relief until the disease spends itself and they recover, or until their sufferings are cut short by death.

There is no farm life, no country life, in India which can be compared with or is in any respect similar to the farm and country life of America. The land is owned by a few wealthy natives. No poor workingman is able to own a foot of land in

his own right.   He rents his farm, which is measured by feet or by rods and not by acres.   He also
rents a tiny room, ten by ten feet square, or twelve
by twelve, in some village near by, where all the
farmers or country folk like himself are crowded
together as closely as they are found in the great
cities.   The farm which they have rented is not
large enough to afford them room for a dwelling,
and even if it were, they dare not live upon it on
account of the many venomous serpents which infest the jungles and the wild beasts which prowl
about.   Early in the morning these farmers, with
their wives, sons, and daughters, all who are old
enough to work, go to the little patch of ground
which they have rented and there they labor during
the whole day, tilling the soil or gathering the grain
according to the season of the year.   With the
crudest kind of plow, merely two sticks fastened
together, and with the help of two bullocks, the sod
is broken up, and the wheat, rice, gram, or other
seed is sown.   Even if the season is favorable and
the harvest abundant, the poor farmer realizes
but a meager sum for his labor, as a large percent-
age of his crop must go to his landlord to pay the
yearly rental for his mud hut and small piece of
ground.

During the night the villagers for the most part
sleep on the ground out of doors, in the roads,
alleys, and lanes of their small country village as it
is too hot in the tiny little room which constitutes
their home, and which has no window or other

means of ventilation except the one door, and in which the family cooking has been done during the evening.

In some parts of India, in Bengal at least, it sometimes happens that while the villagers are sound asleep on the ground their babies, one, two, three, or more, are carried off by a pack of jackals, which have approached the village without arousing the sleepers and snatched away the wee infants before their parents were aware of their presence. Of course the jackals are soon pursued, and in making their flight the infants are dropped, usually badly bitten, scratched, and torn. These infants, torn and bleeding from the teeth and claws of the jackals, are sometimes brought to the missionary evangelist, who tenderly dresses the wounds, inserting stitches where necessary, and bandaging the lacerated limbs as well as possible with the materials at hand.

When in such a village as this the news is circulated that the white-faced missionaries are approaching, a few of its leading citizens will start out on foot to meet the distinguished guests, who are usually tendered a cordial welcome and treated with royal courtesy by these simple country folk. The sick people are brought to him for treatment, and while he ministers to their needs and a few suffering ones are relieved, even in part, his fame spreads abroad and he is reckoned to be well-nigh a god. Early in the morning he begins his song and prayer service in the open air or under the shade of a tree. This soon gives place to the preaching of the Gospel, which continues during all the cool part of the day and late into the night, interspersed with Gospel hymns, prayer, and care of the sick. Sometimes a few only are convinced of the truth of the Christian religion, renounce their idols, profess their faith, and are baptized by the traveling missionary. In some cases, however, a few of the leading members of the community are converted to God, and then the revival spreads until the whole village have turned from their idols and accepted the Lord Jesus Christ as their Saviour, Redeemer, and Friend. In either case, whether only a few or many have been converted to God, it is necessary to establish here a native Christian church, to send a missionary to this village who may live among the people, conduct regular religious services, and instruct these people further in the Christian faith, which they have so recently espoused. Of course they are as yet very ignorant and know but little concerning God's word or his great plan of salvation. If left without further instruction, help, and sympathy, the probabilities are that those already converted will be persuaded by their heathen friends to return to their heathen belief and idol worship. A great difficulty confronts the Missionary Society of the Methodist Episcopal Church in such cases as this. It is impossible to send a thoroughly equipped and qualified missionary to each village of this sort. The regular American missionaries of the parent board and also of the Woman's Foreign Missionary Society

12

are too few in number to supply such appointments as these. They cannot be spared from the more important and responsible positions which they fill in the great centers. We have many native missionary assistants—pastor-teachers, local preachers, exhorters, catechists, Bible readers, zenana workers, etc.—but all of these are, for the most part, fully employed. The policy which has been pursued in cases like the above is that of sending to these villages a native Christian zenana worker, Bible reader, catechist, or pastor-teacher; some one, the best available, who is superior in education and Christian character to the people for whom he or she is to labor. This is the best economy, and it is the only thing to be done under existing circumstances; and yet it must be apparent to all that these country villages where the people have but recently been converted to God and are still without knowledge, education in divine things, or strength of Christian character—the veriest "babes in Christ"—sorely need the help and instruction of a strong missionary. What is to be done? Unless the Church awaken to the need and send help speedily—more missionaries and more money—the cause of God must suffer and much of the ground already gained will be lost. Who is God's steward? Let him hear the call and obey. Perhaps there is no missionary work in India which is more interesting, more engrossing, more full of promise, and altogether more encouraging than this evangelistic work. It has, however, many hindrances, many difficulties, and

The New Missionary and her Moonshee

many disadvantages. It cannot be carried on during all parts of the year. The intense heat of the hot season and the rain of the monsoon render these tours hazardous, if not impossible.

While this evangelistic work is carried on in some denominations by evangelists whose work is confined to this field, it is not by any means peculiar to them. The regular missionary of the parent board, the assistant missionary of the parent board, the zenana missionary of the Woman's Foreign Missionary Society, the teacher missionary of the Woman's Foreign Missionary Society, and the medical missionary of both boards at times engage in this evangelistic work. Indeed, many of them make regular and stated evangelistic tours to the country villages surrounding their missionary homes.

MISSIONARIES OF THE WOMAN'S FOREIGN MISSIONARY SOCIETY OF THE METHODIST EPISCOPAL CHURCH

WOMAN'S work in India embraces zenana teaching, Sunday schools, high schools, normal schools, boarding schools, orphanages, village or evangelistic work, medical missions (including hospitals, dispensaries, training schools for nurses, etc.), and every department of Christian work found in America or in any Christian country.

There are three distinct classes of missionaries sent to India by the Woman's Foreign Missionary

Society of the Methodist Episcopal Church—the teacher missionary, the zenana missionary, and the medical missionary.

Like the regular male missionary of the parent board, each of these lady missionaries must first master, more or less perfectly, one of the many languages spoken by the peoples of Hindustan. To do this one year is usually allowed, during which time the "new" missionary makes her home in an established mission in some center, where she renders whatever assistance she may be able in connection with the general work of the mission, meanwhile pursuing her study of the language which she has selected. Of course everything is new and strange to her, but the zenana teacher or medical missionary with whom she is making her temporary home is always willing and glad to do her part toward initiating the newcomer, and so she progresses, by gradual and easy steps, in her study of the vernacular and also in knowledge of regular missionary methods.

After *chhota haziri*, at about five or six o'clock in the morning, the new missionary, rested and looking fresh in her thin white dress, may be seen with her books and pencil, sitting on the shady side of the house in the deep veranda, in company with her *moonshee* (the native Mohammedan who teaches the Hindustani language), or *pundit* (the Brahmin who instructs you in Marathee or Gujarathee). She is struggling with one of these strange foreign tongues, and will continue her study for one, two, or three hours.

A Moonshee (Mohammedan Teacher)

We need not disturb her. Here she spends her mornings every day with her teacher until she become sufficiently proficient in the language of her choice to take charge of an independent mission.

THE MISSIONARY TEACHER OF THE WOMAN'S FOREIGN MISSIONARY SOCIETY

HAVING passed the required examination in the vernacular, our new missionary teacher now takes over charge of the school or schools to which she has been appointed by the Woman's Foreign Missionary Society. It may be that the teacher previously in charge has been removed by death, or has been obliged to return to America on sick leave, and this new missionary has been appointed to fill the vacant place. Otherwise it may be that the field to which she has been appointed is a new one and the school has not yet been organized. In the latter case she rents a *bungalow* (large English residence), with a more or less extensive *compound* (grounds) surrounding it. The location of this building is a matter of considerable importance, as it is to serve the double purpose of a missionary home and a Christian girls' boarding school. It must not be too far from the native Christian church nor too near to the native city. It should be, above all things, situated in a healthful part of the English town.

Correct legal papers of agreement must be drawn

up between the native landlord and the missionary
teacher, otherwise there may be, later on, dispute
and disagreement as to the monthly rental agreed
upon between the parties. When feasible, however, this property is purchased by the mission, in
which case any such misunderstanding with native
landlord is obviated and many advantages are
gained. In either case the house must now be furnished. In some parts of India the floors will be
matted by native men, who bring to the house the
raw material, reed-grass or split bamboo, braid it
to fit each particular room, and put it down as fast
as it is ready.

Heavy furniture for the house may be rented or
purchased. Often second-hand furniture is purchased at very reasonable rates.

Servants are engaged even before the house is
furnished. The news is soon spread abroad that an
American missionary lady is establishing a home,
and servants come from all directions presenting
their credentials and seeking service. Domingo,
the cook, is the first necessity; then come the "*boot-
lair*" (butler), and the *hamal*, who washes dishes,
cleans lamps, dusts furniture, attends the door, etc. ;
the *dhobie* (laundryman), *ayah* (chambermaid and
nurse), the *malee* (gardener), and the *bihishti* (water
carrier). There is always difficulty in securing the
service of competent, trustworthy, and efficient
servants in the beginning. It requires experience
to enable one to examine the credentials and to
judge correctly as to the qualifications of each serv-

ant; but soon or late the new missionary will be almost certain to find the kind of servants that she needs, and such as will remain with her for years.

When the house is properly furnished and settled, and the servants have adjusted themselves to their several duties and learned the wishes and methods of their new mistress, and all things have been made clean and sweet and wholesome, the pupils begin to gather from all directions, some even coming from distant towns and villages. They are the children of native Christian parents, and are taken into this American Christian home as boarders and inmates. Some of the children are orphans, and are adopted by the mission. Others are half orphans, and are given to the mission by the one surviving parent.

The next necessity which arises is that of engaging competent native Christian teachers for each of the various departments in this growing school. These are usually chosen from the advanced pupils in the older Methodist girls' boarding schools in other parts of India. These Christian teachers may be of native (Hindustan or Mohammedan), Eurasian, or English parentage. The majority of these assistant teachers are Eurasian and wear English dress, but they all live in European style and sit at the same table with the American missionary who has established the home, organized the school, and who presides as mistress, chief teacher, superintendent, mother, and friend. It devolves upon her to decide all matters of importance and to maintain strict discipline among both pupils and teachers. She determines at what hour they shall all retire to rest at night, at what hour they shall arise in the morning, how much time shall be given to recreation, how much to study, and what proportion shall be devoted to domestic service. All letters coming to and going from this home must be first opened and read by her.

The children in this school are required to live in native style. There are no chairs or benches in the recitation room or rooms. The children all sit upon the floor in real oriental style, with legs crossed and heads bowed. They are all attired in pure white sari, and none of them are allowed to speak the English language or to take up English studies until after they have passed the matriculation examination in their own native tongue. At night they all sleep together in a large dormitory, or, if the school be large, there may be several of these. In some well-established schools these little native children are provided with native cots. In many cases they are not allowed this luxury, but each little girl wraps her sari about her in native style, and lies down to rest upon a hay mattress or a folded comfortable on the floor. In some schools the children do all, or nearly all, the domestic work. They live on native food, curry and rice, principally. This they cook themselves, the girls taking turns by the day or by the week. They laundry their own sari, have entire charge of the dormitories and schoolrooms, and in many cases serve the missionary and her staff of

The Girls' Boarding School of the Woman's Foreign Missionary Society, Bombay, India

teachers at table, washing the dishes afterward, and doing many other domestic services in the missionary home.

Of course it is impossible to describe minutely the exact kind and amount of work which devolves upon pupils in these schools, as each particular school has rules peculiar to itself. Indeed, in some of the Church of England mission schools, and perhaps in those of other denominations also, it is not expected of the pupils that they do any domestic work in the apartments of the missionary or of the teachers. In all such schools, however, the pupils are taught ordinary cooking and everything which pertains to the care of an Indian woman's home; and each little girl is required to do her own sewing. In some schools the wheat is purchased unground and the little girls are required to grind it, according to native custom, in the early morning, with the native mill, such as was used in Bible times.

In addition to this they have their regular hours for study, for recitation, and for play. On the Sabbath day they all march together, headed by their teacher or teachers, to the regular services of the native Christian church and to Sabbath school.

In addition to the care and superintendency of this home and boarding school by our missionary teacher of the Woman's Foreign Missionary Society, there may be several girls' day schools in the native city which she superintends and has entire management of, such as those we have described above

as being under the care of the regular male missionary of the parent board.

The policy of keeping the pupils in these native
Christian girls' boarding schools in native costume
and requiring them to live in native style is based
upon two conditions and has two objects in view,
namely, in cases where these girls continue in
school a sufficient length of time to qualify them to
serve as Bible readers, zenana workers, or assistant
teachers their salary must of necessity be small, and
in no case can it be sufficient to maintain them in
comfortable English homes provided with chairs,
tables, beds, and all the furniture, crockery, pictures, etc., which go to make up an ordinary English or American home. It will be, however, sufficiently large to maintain them comfortably in native
style. If during school life they are taught to live
in English style, with all the luxuries of English
home life, they will become discontented, restive,
and unhappy under the privations that must be
theirs in future life. In case these pupils marry,
before or after the conclusion of their school course,
the result is the same. They must marry native or
Eurasian men, who receive a salary far too small
to maintain them comfortably in English style.

The second principle upon which this policy is
based involves, to the Missionary Society, a question
of economy. The amount of money in the missionary treasury is not sufficient to educate a large number of pupils, if they are to be maintained in English
style during their school days. There is a very

large number of children of native Christian parentage who desire the advantages of Christian education, but whose parents are able to pay little or nothing for it.   There is also a large number of orphans or half orphans to whom a Christian boarding school is a boon indeed.   The question to be considered is, simply, is it better, with the means available, to receive into our girls' boarding schools a small number of pupils, to whom we will supply all the comforts (to them luxuries) of a properly equipped American girls' boarding school, or, on the other hand, shall we maintain these native girls in native style—thereby economizing our money—and thus make it possible to accommodate a very much larger number of pupils?   On all accounts it is deemed wiser to follow the latter policy; and thus our mission schools are crowded with pupils, and large numbers of native girls who otherwise must remain in ignorance are housed, clothed, taught, and fitted for lives of usefulness and independence.

THE ZENANA MISSIONARY OF THE WOMAN'S FOREIGN MISSIONARY SOCIETY

WHEN the zenana missionary has completed her term of apprenticeship, and has successfully passed the Conference examination in the vernacular, she is given over charge of the independent mission to which she has been appointed by the Woman's Foreign Missionary Society.

As in the case of our teacher missionary, this
may be an old, well-established mission left vacant
by death or removal, or it may be a new field where
she is expected to establish zenana mission work.
In the latter case, property suited to the purpose
which she has in view must be rented or purchased,
servants engaged, furniture secured, and native or
Eurasian zenana missionary assistants engaged.

These assistants are usually called from older
missions in other parts of India, and are taken, as
were the assistant teachers, from among the senior
pupils of our native Christian girls' boarding
schools.

To each of these assistant zenana workers a
stipend of ten rupees per month, with board, is
considered a good and sufficient salary. In some
missions, however, a less sum than this is paid and
in some a larger amount.

In these zenana missionary homes *chhota haziri* is
usually served at five, five-thirty, or six o'clock in
the morning, the zenana missionary and her assistants coming down to the dining room and partaking
of their little breakfast together as any other meal
is served. Immediately after the tea and toast the
missionary and her assistants drive to the native
city in their missionary wagon or carriage, a large
covered rig, accommodating six or eight persons.
Arriving at some central point in the native city,
or driving up and down through the narrow streets,
the zenana workers separate, each going to her
respective zenana home where she is to instruct the

zenana women. She is supposed to teach these women knitting, sewing, fancywork, reading, writing, spelling, and all the rudiments of an ordinary education. Her principal object, however, is to teach them the truths of our holy Christian religion; and with this end in view the Bible is her chief text-book. She may have several pupils in one home. Perhaps the master of the house has several wives; he also may have several sons who are married, and his daughters-in-law make their home with him.

All natives of India are bitterly prejudiced against Christian missionaries. They believe them to be spies and proselyters who have been hired by the English or American government to come to India for the express purpose of breaking the caste of the native and of leading away his wife and daughter from their home, from their religious belief, from their caste, and from all that they hold sacred. He holds the Englishman in awe and ostensible respect, as his master and conqueror, but at heart he hates and despises him. He knows very little about the American, but likes him better than the Englishman on general principles, not knowing why.

Nevertheless, he has, after much persuasion, consented to allow the zenana missionary to visit his wives and daughters at stated hours on certain days of the week, regularly, for the purpose of teaching them. Why does he do this? His women folk are too high-caste and too wealthy to be allowed to soil their hands with work. They have servants who wait upon them—bathing the person, dressing the hair, and making the toilet altogether. They cannot read or write. Many of them have never seen a paper or a book. They are not allowed to go outside of the four great walls which surround his courtyard. There is no variety in their lives, no change to break the dull monotony. They see no strange faces, they hear little or no news, they have little to think about except their own miseries and ailments. Therefore they naturally grow restive, irritable, jealous, and hysterical. They think so much about every ache and pain as to develop each particular ache and pain into a disease, in their distorted imagination. Thus this wealthy man's family becomes troublesome. He is tried and driven to his wit's end, not knowing what to do with or for his women folk. He hears about the zenana missionary lady. He fears her, distrusts her, and perhaps even despises her; but she would teach his wives and his daughters-in-law fancywork; she would amuse and interest them; she would serve as a new toy (they never have any toys), and so he decides to allow the zenana missionary to make regular visits to his home for the purpose of instructing his wives and daughters-in-law. Before consenting to visit his home, however, our zenana missionary stipulates that she be allowed to teach the Bible to the women of the household. This, also, he finally agrees to, but takes precaution against its consequences.

A Wealthy High-caste Zenana Lady of Bombay

He instructs his wives and daughters that he has invited the zenana missionary lady from America or from England to visit them; that she will teach them how to sew, how to knit, how to embroider, and how to do all sorts of beautiful fancywork. Then he tells them that she is a spy and a proselyter, and that they must beware of her; that she has been hired by the English or American government to come to India for the purpose of robbing them of their religious beliefs, idols, home, friends, and caste. He assures them that he has consented for her to visit them in order that they may learn the fancywork and because he feels that he can trust them. They must not believe anything she may tell them about her Christian religion; they must not believe the Bible she reads to them, because it is all false and will lead them astray. Thus are the minds of the little native women poisoned and prejudiced against their zenana missionary teacher before they have ever seen her face. The day for her visit is arranged for, the hour appointed, and all the little women of the native household are in readiness for her reception. They have donned their best silk garments and wear all their jewels. They are in a flutter of excitement in anticipation of the strange guest.

Of course they tender her a most warm and cordial reception. A native woman is always dignified, always courteous, the very soul of politeness; she is incapable of rudeness.

The zenana missionary does little in the way of

teaching on the occasion of her first visit; she must first become personally acquainted with her pupils. She makes herself generally agreeable, answering all their questions, the first of which will probably be, "How old are you?" Then, "Are you married?" If she answer in the negative, they do not believe her. It is incredible to the native of India that any man or woman should arrive at the age of maturity unmarried. If she answer in the affirmative, the next question is, "How many children have you?" All questions are answered kindly. The zenana missionary allows her new pupils to examine the buttons on her dress, her breastpin, her cuffs, and all the details of her European costume. This is not considered rude among Indians, and, of course, English dress is a great curiosity in such a home as this. When she becomes a little better acquainted some of the younger women may take down her hair and toy with it as she goes on with her lesson. They are sweet, gentle women, with a delicate sense of propriety and a dignity so innate, so pretty, and so genuine that even the most refined American or English woman is liable to feel some strange sense of embarrassment in the presence of a company of such charming creatures; for, indeed, they are charming in person and in manner, and as you come to know them intimately you will find that they are just as sweet and just as charming in character, except for the strange heathen beliefs and prejudices, which are the fault of their birthplace and surroundings rather than their own.

The new teacher finds her pupils bright, intelligent, quick to learn, and altogether interesting. They ask eager questions and remember readily. They have intelligent minds and are able to reason out and to answer; so that the zenana worker must be a clever woman in order to give them logical and reasonable answers and conclusions to their arguments. When the heat becomes intense, at half past nine, ten, ten-thirty, or eleven o'clock A. M., according to the season of the year and the part of India where this work is being carried on, our zenana missionary workers gather into the missionary carriage and return to their home, where breakfast is in waiting. After breakfast family prayers are conducted, the servants attending, as in the case of the regular missionary of the parent board. Breakfast and family worship over, the zenana missionary gives instruction to the servants as to the household duties of the day, meets her zenana missionary assistants, instructs them as to their various tasks, or listens to the report of each. After this she repairs to her room for the purpose of letter or report writing. At one or two o'clock P. M. *tiffin* is served, after which the zenana missionary and her assistants may have a Bible reading together or a prayer service, or they may take a rest for half an hour or so.

At four, four-thirty, or five o'clock P. M. the missionary carriage again waits in front of our zenana missionary *bungalow*, and presently the zenana missionary and her assistants start out again for other

13

zenana homes, where they are to teach, and from which they do not return until six, seven, or eight o'clock in the evening, according to the season of the year and to the part of India in which they are living.

After their return the butler announces, "*Khana taiyar hai, Miss Sahib*" (Dinner is ready, Miss Sir). After dinner there may be a church service to attend, or the zenana missionary may meet her assistants, hear their reports, and instruct them in the best methods of expounding the Holy Scriptures and of winning the souls of zenana women to Christ.

In the beginning the work of the zenana missionary is very disheartening, but as these earnest, consecrated women persevere, going from house to house and spending one, two, or three hours daily in each home, teaching these poor, imprisoned, but really gentle and lovely women the truths of our blessed Gospel, the seed is sown in good ground and must ere long bring forth an abundant harvest. The minds of these zenana women are far too fertile, their judgment too clear, and their reasoning faculties too bright for them to be long deceived. The day comes when their judgments are convinced of the truth of the Christian religion, and when this at length happens there is no more rest for the little woman until she has taken up her cross, left all, and followed Christ. It means much for her to do this, but she has the courage of her convictions. Her mind is no sooner convinced than her heart responds, and she soon becomes willing

to sacrifice all that she may gain Christ. She announces to her husband and family the fact that she
has espoused the cause of her Lord Jesus Christ and
fully believes in the Christian religion, and wishes
to become a Christian herself. It is a bold thing
for her to make such an announcement in her
heathen home. The zenana missionary teacher is
now advised that her visits must be discontinued.
The little pupil is locked up in a small, dark room
and is scourged with many stripes daily in the hope
that she will soon renounce her new faith and declare her intention of returning to the faith of her
family. This, however, she does not do. She is
firm. She bears her torture with fortitude, in silence,
and with the utmost patience receives all harsh
words and cruel treatment. She is, perhaps, half
starved and obliged to suffer unutterable tortures.
Alone, without the zenana missionary teacher, who
has come to be her truest friend, without the privilege of making known her sufferings to any sympa-
thizing soul, she weeps and prays in her dark and
solitary room. Finally, however, she makes her
escape, or perhaps is beaten, kicked, and thrust out
into the street at the dead of night because she will
not yield. She is a stranger in the outside world.
She never before stood on the street of a city outside the high walls of her husband's house. All
seems strange to her, and she is timid and alarmed.
At length, however, in her fear and desperation, she
inquires of some passing woman the way to the missionary *bungalow*. Everybody knows where it is,

the zenana missionary home, and she is soon directed aright. With fear and trembling she makes her way to the home of her teacher friend. At last she stands at the door, her heart throbbing with mingled feelings of fear and joy. Timidly she knocks, and is ushered into the presence of her teacher, at whose feet she falls, convulsed with sobs. She soon tells her story, and is allowed to remain in the missionary home, at least for the present. Perhaps her friends will come for her within a few hours and tear her away by force, only to renew their beatings and starvation, or perhaps they will allow her to remain with the zenana missionary, threatening her life if she should ever return to her home or be found seeking an interview with any member of her husband's family. If she be a mother, she can never see her children again. Her family consider that she has disgraced them all, broken her caste, and ruined herself and them.

In the Church of England Zenana Missionary Home, of Krishnagar, Bengal, there are ten, twelve, or more of these women, who have either been violently driven from their homes in the manner above described or who have made their escape by stealth, and who are now glad to labor in any way to maintain themselves while they study the blessed Gospel of Jesus Christ, with the hope that some day they may be able to go to the women of their own caste and instruct them in the blessed religion which they have espoused and for which they have suffered so much and forsaken all else.

A Zenana Missionary of the Methodist Episcopal Church and Her Assistants in Bombay

I was in that home when one of these little women, who had been separated from her three children for a period of three or four years, was permitted to meet her eldest son. During all these years she had never seen any member of her family, except her father, who paid her occasional visits. Her mother-heart longed for her children, and whenever her father came to see her she had begged him to bring her children that she might look into their faces once again. Her father invariably refused this request, but at length he did bring her eldest son, and I had the privilege of witnessing that sad, glad meeting. The little woman was too overjoyed for words. She pressed her firstborn to her heart and wept and wept until everybody present was in tears. Her father allowed the son to remain with his mother for one half hour only, having previously stipulated that not a word should be spoken in regard to the Christian religion. At the expiration of the half hour the parting came, and it was so sad and full of pain to both parties that we could not help doubting whether it were not better for her never to see her son rather than to see him for so short a time and under such restrictions.

Do not suppose from the above that the zenana missionary seeks to break up the home of the native zenana woman, or that she endeavors by any means to induce her to forsake home and family. On the contrary, the zenana missionary makes use of every effort in her power, every argument and every influence she possesses, to bring about harmony between the zenana woman who has declared her faith in the Christian religion and her heathen family, and to establish peace in the zenana home. Failing in this, when the heathen parents, husband, and friends of the little woman, feeling outraged and disgraced by her change of faith, torture, beat, and starve her until her life is imperiled, and she, in her desperation, makes her escape from her place of torture and imprisonment and flees for refuge to the missionary home, or is thrust out from her home violently, perhaps in the dead of night, and afterward finds her way to the zenana missionary *bungalow;* in such cases as these the missionary extends to her not only sympathy and words of advice, comfort, and tenderness, but gladly gives her the shelter and protection which she so much needs.

THE MEDICAL MISSIONARY OF THE WOMAN'S FOREIGN MISSIONARY SOCIETY

LIKE the teacher and the zenana missionary, the medical missionary of the Woman's Foreign Missionary Society must serve as an apprentice in some well-established medical mission for a year or more, studying the native language, acquainting herself with the methods of medical mission work, and becoming familiar with the diseases peculiar to India and with their treatment.

At the expiration of this time, having passed the required Conference examinations, she is appointed to an independent medical mission, where, perhaps, she takes over charge of a missionary hospital for women and children, a missionary dispensary for women and children, and a medical missionary training school for nurses; or it may be, as in the case of the teacher and zenana missionaries, that there is a new field, and the hospital, dispensary, and training school for nurses are to be started, organized, and established by herself. In the latter case, after the property for the medical mission has been selected and rented or purchased, the house or houses furnished, the servants engaged, and all things put in order, native and Eurasian women, old and young, gather from all directions, applying to be received as student nurses in this medical missionary training school. It requires considerable tact, skill, and judgment to discriminate wisely between these applicants, and to receive into the school only the most intelligent and trustworthy—such as will develop into efficient and reliable medical assistants.

These student nurses, for the most part, are wholly without education. Some of them, perhaps, are native midwives, versed in all the barbarous treatments and remedial agents employed by the unlettered heathen doctors in cases of confinement as well as in medical and surgical cases. To disabuse their ignorant, prejudiced, and superstitious minds of all the errors already learned is a stupendous task, and yet it is more important that these midwives be " unlearned " the false principles which they have acquired, and taught scientific and proper treatment, than that others, who make no profession of skill in the treatment of diseases or in the management of confinement cases, be instructed. For the latter, making no pretensions to knowledge or skill, are harmless, while the native midwife is a most dangerous individual, not only inflicting unutterable torture upon the poor victims who are intrusted to her care, but often and often causing premature death both to mother and child through her barbarous and cruel practices.

Our medical missionary is fortunate if she have an associate medical missionary to share her labors and responsibilities, or even a properly trained and efficient nurse. Without these her burdens are heavy indeed. She has the entire charge of her missionary home, hospital, dispensary, and training school for nurses. The native servants are not taught antiseptic measures and know nothing about medical and surgical cleanliness. The medical missionary, therefore, must carefully guard every patient under her charge, else contagion, infection, septic fever, puerperal fever, cholera, smallpox, or leprosy may develop in the wards of her hospital, and run such a violent course as to necessitate the closing up of the institution.

Her ignorant heathen nurses in training, with no principles of honor or morality to shield them from temptation, must be guarded and shielded and watched over by the medical missionary with the utmost and most unremitting care. They must, of course, receive daily instruction. They cannot read, and if they are to become even moderately efficient, trustworthy nurses, they must be taught daily, minutely, and continuously by word of mouth. This involves almost incessant toil on the part of our medical missionary, to say nothing of the patients in the hospital, in the office, and in the dispensary, whose health and whose lives are almost wholly dependent upon her skill, wisdom, and careful management. If she be not on her guard, acutely watchful, and intensely vigilant, some native midwife, now a student nurse in her school, will administer some fatal remedy to one of her patients —perhaps an overdose of laudanum to a wee infant —or she will practice some barbarous cruelty upon a patient in labor, or will poison the minds of her high-caste native patients toward her. Some suspicion as to the medicine, instruments, or medical methods of the institution will arise, and increase until a veritable panic occur, and perhaps all the patients withdraw from the hospital in a single hour.

The free missionary dispensary claims a certain proportion of the medical missionary's time, strength, and thought. Certain hours in each day are given to this work. There she receives, examines, and treats fifty, eighty, or even one or two hundred patients daily, according to the age of her establishment, size of the city, etc.

No precaution is taken by the natives of India against contagion, and, in spite of all efforts on the

part of the medical missionary to avoid the consequences of such a condition, cases of smallpox,
leprosy, and cholera are often brought to her dispensary for treatment.

Other missionaries may so adjust their hours of
work as to be indoors and under the *punkah* during
the intense heat of the midday sun; the medical
missionary, however, has no choice. She must go
when she is called. It may be that at the noon
hour she will be summoned to the sick couch of a
high-caste or low-caste, rich or poor, native woman,
who resides in the very heart of the native city.
She dons her pith helmet, takes a huge umbrella
lined with green and covered with white muslin,
and drives in her close carriage to the home of the
sufferer. The native streets are very narrow, the
gutters on either side open, the rays of the sun intolerable, and the stench oppressive; one's life is
imperiled by such exposure. Perhaps she must
remain in the close, dark, small apartment of her
patient during all the long hours of that hot summer
day. Perhaps she is obliged to remain far into the
night, toiling on without food or rest, struggling to
maintain the life of her patient. Meanwhile she is
anxious and troubled as to the work at home. She
does not know what mischief may be done during
her absence. Perhaps she returns in the early
morning. She must now bathe and change her apparel, to avoid any possibility of contagion to her
patients and nurses. It is then time for *chhota
haziri*, and immediately after this the numerous

duties of her busy life press in upon her.   It is impossible for her to take the rest so sorely needed, nor is it certain that she will have an opportunity to retire to rest on the following night.   Indeed, it often happens that two or three such nights succeed one another.

In the office, in the hospital, and in the dispensaries, while the medical missionary is examining patients, prescribing for them, administering treatment, or performing operations, the other patients who have gathered in the reception room and who are awaiting their turn are being entertained by one of the native Christian nurses or Bible women, as she reads and expounds the Holy Scriptures, prays, and sings; and each one, as she passes into the consulting room, receives a tract or a portion of the New Testament in her own native tongue.

Thus are medical and mission work carried on together, the medical serving as a means whereby the missionary may gain access to the hearts, homes, sympathies, and confidence of the natives.   The native of India is not prejudiced against lady physicians, though he is bitterly prejudiced against missionaries.   It seems never to have dawned upon the native understanding that a woman may be both a physician and a missionary.   In his time of need, therefore, when wife, mother, daughter, or young son is ill and suffering, perhaps nigh unto death, he sends with all speed for the medical woman; and not until she has won his respect, confidence, and perhaps affection does he realize that his physician is also a missionary.

When the work of the medical missionary is well established, and she has spent some years in India, she will be almost certain to establish several missionary dispensaries in the native city. These she will visit herself as often as possible, and always manage and superintend, but for the most part they will be under the daily care and direction of her senior student nurses. The medical missionary must be a woman of superior ability, capable of managing a variety of interests at one time and a large number of people.

In addition to having the entire charge, management, and superintendency of a large missionary home and center, a missionary hospital for women and children, one, two, three, or more missionary dispensaries for women and children in the native city, she is also a medical missionary teacher, having a class of ignorant, untutored native women in her home, to whom she must give medical and nurse lectures and quizzes every day, besides an occasional oral examination. She is also a private practitioner of medicine, having a more or less extensive office and out practice; and, in addition to all this, she can never forget that she is preeminently and above all things a missionary. In her home, in her hospital, in her dispensaries, in her office, among her student nurses, and in the bedchamber of her out-patients she is at once the friend, the teacher, the physician, and the missionary, pointing pupils and patients to "the Lamb of God, which taketh away the sin of the world." Kneeling in prayer on the ground floor in the little dark apartment of some poor patient, quoting a passage of Scripture to some suffering woman, singing a hymn in the death chamber, and thus following in the footsteps of the great First Medical Missionary, who left his Father's throne and came to earth "to seek and to save that which was lost," going about healing all manner of diseases, teaching and preaching the Gospel unto the poor.

In some cases, where the mission is young and weak, the school, zenana, and medical work are consolidated, forming one only, instead of three independent missions. In other cases, where the mission is old and well established, there may be two or three associate zenana missionaries, together with a large number of native and Eurasian assistant zenana workers, in connection with one zenana mission, two or three associate missionary teachers in one missionary school, besides a large staff of native and Eurasian assistant missionary teachers and two or three associate medical missionaries in connection with one medical mission, also a large and efficient staff of native and Eurasian hospital assistants and student nurses.

The author has had the privilege of enjoying the hospitality of several missionary homes, such as are described in the foregoing pages. She was one of the first inmates, a guest and boarder, in the Zenana Mission of the Woman's Foreign Missionary Society in Bombay, and knew something of the burdens, struggles, anxieties, and almost innumerable difficulties which confronted her dear friend, Miss S. De Line, the zenana missionary of the Woman's Foreign Missionary Society, in her efforts to establish a permanent zenana mission in that great city, and to do it in such a manner as would prove the greatest possible success and a blessing to India. She was intimately familiar with the everyday home life and labors of the two beautiful and noble women, Miss Alice Aitken and Miss Nellie Reddies, of the Normal School Instruction Society of Lahore, Punjab. She was a patient in St. Catherine's Hospital of the Medical Mission of the Church Missionary Society of Amritsar, Punjab, where the peerless trio, the Misses Sarah Hewlett, E. S. Bartlett, and A. Sharp, preside with such grace, womanly dignity and strength, carrying on a most extensive medical mission, comprising a hospital, several missionary dispensaries in the native city, and an important medical missionary training school for nurses. She was also a guest during a long season of convalescence in the Church of England Zenana Mission House of Krishnagar, Bengal, where Miss Tharp (now Mrs. Tharp Gill) and Miss Eleanor M. Sampson reigned queens, as they truly are, in a home which was in every respect a perfect Christian home and missionary center. She knows whereof she speaks, therefore, when she affirms that there are no homes anywhere to be found which excel the missionary home in the observance of regular, methodical, systematic order in the careful husbanding of time, in mutual kindness and consideration each for the other—" in honor preferring one another."   Than missionaries of the Gospel there can be no Christians more self-forgetting, self-sacrificing, devout, earnest, zealous, forbearing, always abounding in good works, devoted to the cause of the Master, efficient in his service, and intelligently consecrated in all their lives—whose " works do follow them."

Pray for the heroes and heroines of Zion !

CONCLUSION

GOD'S own ambassadors and yours
Have tried each pass,
But may not enter where
The money king holds sway.
Not many mighty ones are called,
Not many wise ; so are we taught
In God's own blessed word.
The poor must have the Gospel
Preached to them.
The Lord hath chosen them,
The weak, the things of naught,
To bring to naught the things that are.
The lowly ones are chosen first,
And grow to stalwart sons and
Daughters of the living God.
He sends them forth to lift his
Banner high—to sound abroad
The triumphs of their risen Lord—
Full seven times to blow the trump
Of God and shout at his command :
When, lo ! the prison walls

Shall fall and crumble into dust,
As if by fire consumed.
And do you look with
Longing eye and eager heart
To see this glad fruition?
Then give with cheerful hand
From out your hoarded store,
And watch and pray the more,
For God will surely hear
And answer prayer.

September 29, 1897.

THE END.